Rico And Wiseli

Johanna Spyri

Contents

RICO AND WISELI

BY

Johanna Spyri

RICO AND STINELI.

CHAPTER I.
IN THE QUIET HOUSE.

In the Ober Engadin, on the highway up to Maloja, stands the lonely village of Sils; and back towards the mountains, across the fields, nestles a little cluster of huts known as Sils Maria. Here, in an open field, two cottages stand, facing each other.

Noticeable in both are the old wooden house-doors, and the tiny windows quite imbedded in the thick walls. A bit of a garden-plot belongs to one of these poor dwellings, where the pot-herbs and the cabbages look only a trifle better than their spindling companions the flowers.

The other house has nothing but a little shed, where two or three hens may be seen running in and out. This cottage is smaller than its neighbor, and its wooden door is quite black from age.

Out of this door every morning, at the same hour, came a large man. In order to pass out he was obliged to stoop, so tall was he. His hair was black and glossy, and his eyes were also black; and under his finely-shaped nose grew a thick black beard, completely hiding the lower part of his face; so that, except the glistening of his white teeth when he spoke, nothing was visible. But he rarely spoke.

Everybody in Sils knew the man, but he was never called by his name,--it was always "the Italian." He went by the foot-path across to Sils every day regularly, and thence up to Maloja. They were working on the highway in that place, and there he found employment.

When, however, he did not have work up there, he went down to the Baths of

St. Moritz. Houses were being built down there, and he found work in plenty; and there passed the day, only returning to his cottage at nightfall.

When he came out of his house in the morning, he was usually followed by a little boy, who lingered on the threshold after his father had gone on his way, and looked with his big black eyes for a long time in the direction his father had taken; but where he was looking that no one could have told, for his eyes had a faraway look, as if they saw nothing that lay before them and near, but were searching for something invisible to everybody.

On Sunday mornings, when the sun shone brightly, father and son would saunter up the road together; and the close resemblance between them was most striking, for the child was the man in miniature, only his face was small and pale,--with his father's well-formed nose, to be sure; but his mouth had an expression of great sadness, as if he could not laugh. In his father's face this could not be detected, on account of the beard.

When they walked along together, side by side, they did not talk; but the father usually hummed a tune softly,--sometimes quite aloud,--and the lad listened attentively. On rainy Sundays they sat at the window together in the cottage, and seldom talked then; but the man drew his harmonica from his pocket, and played one tune after another to the lad, who listened most earnestly. Sometimes he would take a comb, or even a leaf, and coax forth music; or he would shape a bit of wood with his knife, and whistle a tune upon that. It really seemed as if there were no object from which he could not draw forth sweet sounds. Once, however, he brought a fiddle home with him, and the boy was so delighted with the instrument, that he never forgot it. The man played one tune after another, while the child listened and looked with all his might; and when the fiddle was laid aside, the little fellow took it up, and tried to find out for himself how the music was made. And it could not have sounded so very badly, for his father had smiled, saying, "Come, now!" and placed the big fingers of his left hand over his son's, and held the little hand and the bow together in his right; and thus they played for a long time, and produced a great many sweet tunes.

On the following day, after his father's departure, the boy tried again and again to play, until at last he did succeed in producing a tune quite correctly. Soon after, however, the fiddle disappeared, and never made its appearance again.

Often, when they were together, the man would begin to sing softly,--softly at first, then more and more distinctly as he became more interested, and the boy know the words, he could at least follow the tune. The father sang Italian always; and the child understood a great deal, but not well enough to sing. One tune, however, he knew better than any other, for his father had repeated it many hundred times. It was part of a long song, and began in this wise:--

"One evening In Peschiera."

It was a sad melody that some one had arranged to a pretty ballad, and it particularly pleased the lad, so that he always sang it with pleasure and with a feeling of awe; and it sounded very sweetly, for the lad had a clear, bell-like voice, that harmonized beautifully with his father's strong basso. And each time after they had sung this song from beginning to end, his father clapped the boy kindly on the shoulder, saying, "Well done, Henrico! well done!" This was the way his father called him, but he was called "Rico" only by everybody else.

There was a cousin who lived in the cottage with them, and who mended and cooked and kept the house in order. In the winter she sat by the stove and spun, and Rico had to consider how he could enter the room, very carefully; for as soon as he had opened the door, his cousin called out, "Do let that door alone, or we shall have it cold enough in the room here."

In winter he was very often alone with his cousin; for when his father had work to do in the valley, he would be away for long weeks at a time.

CHAPTER II.
IN THE SCHOOL.

Rico was almost nine years old, and had been to school for two winters. Up there in the mountains there was no school in the summer-time; for then the teacher had his field to cultivate, and his hay and wood to cut, like everybody else, and nobody had time to think of going to school. This was not a great sorrow for Rico,--he knew how to amuse himself. When he had once taken his place in the morning on the threshold, he would stand there for hours without moving, gazing into the far distance with dreamy eyes, if the door of the house over the way did not open, and a little girl make her appearance and look over at him laughingly. Then Rico ran over to her in a trice, and the children were busy enough in telling each other what had happened since the evening before, and talked incessantly, until Stineli was called into the house. The girl's name was Stineli, and she and Rico were of exactly the same age. They began to go to school at the same time, were in the same classes, and from that time forward were always together; for there was only a narrow path between their cottages, and they were the dearest of friends.

This was the only intimacy that Rico had, for he had no pleasure in the companionship of the other boys; and when they thrashed each other, or played at wrestling, or turned somersaults, he went away without even looking back at them. If they called out after him, "Now it is Rico's turn to be thrashed," he stood perfectly still and did nothing; but he looked at them so strangely with his dark eyes, that no one meddled with him.

In Stineli's company he was always contented. She had a merry little pug-nose, and two brown eyes that were always laughing; and around her head were two thick braids of brown hair, that always looked smooth and neat, for Stineli was a very orderly girl, and knew very well how to take care of herself. For that her daily experience was excellent. It is true Stineli was scarcely nine years old, but she was the eldest daughter of the family, and had to help her mother in every thing, and there was a great deal to be done,--for after Stineli came Trudi and Sami and Peterli, then Urschli and Anne-Deteli and Kunzli, and last of all the baby, who was not baptized. From every corner, at every moment, Stineli was called for; and she had become so handy and skilful with all this practice, that work seemed to turn itself out of her hands of its own accord. She could always put on three stockings and fasten two shoes before Trudi had even placed the legs of the little one she was helping in the right position. And while her mother was calling for Stineli to help her in the kitchen, and the little children wanted her in the bedroom, her father was sure to shout out from the stable for Stineli to come to his help, for he had mislaid his cap, or his whip-lash was in a knot, and she found the one in a trice,--it was generally on the meal-box,--and her limber fingers had no trouble in untying the knotted lash. So, you see, Stineli was always busy running about and working, but always merry with it all, and rejoiced also in winter, when the school began. Then she went with Rico to school and back again, and in recess they were also together. And in summer she was still more happy, for then the lovely Sunday evenings came when she could go out; and she and Rico went, hand in hand,--the lad was always waiting for her in the doorway,--over the big meadow towards the wood on the hill-side that projected far out over the lake like an island. They used to sit up there under the pines, and look out over the green waters of the lake, and had so many questions to ask and so many answers to give, and were so happy, that Stineli was happy all the week in thinking it over and looking forward,--for Sunday always came again.

There was yet one other person in the household who called for Stineli now and then,--that was her old grandmother.

She did not want her assistance, however, but had generally a bit of money to give her that she had put aside, or some little thing that would give the girl pleasure; for the grandmother noticed how much there was for Stineli to do, and that she had less pleasure than other children of her age, and the child was her favorite. She always had something ready so that she could buy herself a red ribbon at the yearly market, or a needle-case, if she wished.

Rico was also a favorite with this good grandmother, and she liked to see the children together, and tried to contrive a little recreation for them now and then.

On summer evenings the grandmother always sat by the door on a tree-stump that was there, and often Stineli and Rico stood by her side while she told them stories. But when the prayer-bell sounded from the little church tower she always said, "Now say, 'Our Father;' and be sure, children, that you never forget to say that prayer every evening; the prayer-bells ring to remind you of that." "Now remember, little ones," she would now and then repeat, "I have lived for a long, long time, and had a great deal of experience, and I have never known a single person who has not, at some time or other in his life, sore need of 'Our Father;' but I have known many a one who has sought to say it anxiously, and not found it, in his great need." So Stineli and Rico stood reverently side by side and said their evening prayer.

Now May had come, and there was only a short time to pass before school would cease, for under the trees there were signs of green, and the snow had melted and vanished in many places. Rico had been standing for a long time in the doorway making these welcome observations. At the same time he looked again and again towards the opposite door, hoping that it would open. It did at last, and out came Stineli.

"How long have you been standing there?" she called out merrily. "It is early to-day, and we can go along slowly."

They took each other's hands, and went towards the schoolhouse.

"Are you always thinking about the lake?" asked Stineli as they went along.

"Yes, of course," said Rico, with a serious expression; "and I often dream about it too, and see great red flowers there, and in the distance the purple mountains."

"Oh! what one dreams does not count," said Stineli. "I dreamed once that Peterli climbed, all alone, to the top of the highest pine-tree; and when he was on the top twig, suddenly he changed into a bird and called out, 'Come, Stineli, and put on my stockings for me.' So you see that it does not mean any thing when you dream."

Rico pondered over this, for his dream might certainly mean something, and yet only be thoughts passing through his mind. Now, however, they were near the schoolhouse, and a troop of noisy children came towards them from the opposite direction. They all entered together, and soon the teacher came in. He was an old man with thin, gray hair, for he had been teacher for an incredibly long time,--so long, that his hair had grown gray and fallen out.

Now a busy spelling and pronouncing began; then followed the multiplication-table, and, lastly, the singing. For this the teacher brought out his old fiddle and tuned it. Then they began, and all shouted at the top of their lungs,--

"Little lambkins, come down From the bright sunny height,"

and the teacher played the accompaniment.

Rico, however, had his eyes fixed so attentively upon the fiddle, and on the teacher's fingers as he touched the strings, that he quite forgot the song; and at this the whole choir lost their pitch, and fell away a half-note, and the fiddle became uncertain, and lost a half-note also; and then the voices fell lower still, until at last nobody could have told where they were going to all together; but the teacher tossed his fiddle upon the table and called out angrily, "What sort of a song do you call that? You are nothing but a lot of screamers! I should like to know who it is who sings false and spoils the whole time."

At this a little boy spoke up,--the one who sat nearest to Rico: "I know why it all goes wrong. It always goes that way when Rico stops singing."

The teacher himself knew that the fiddle was somewhat dependent on Rico's leading.

"Rico, Rico! what is this that I hear?" he said, turning to the lad. "You are generally a well-behaved boy; but inattention is a sad fault, as you now see. One single careless scholar can easily spoil a whole song. Now we will begin anew; and be more attentive, Rico."

After this the boy sang with his steady, clear voice; the fiddle followed, and the children sang with all their might, and it went on very satisfactorily to the very end.

The teacher was well satisfied, and rubbed his hands together, and then drew his bow over the string, saying, with a pleased air, "It is a good instrument, after all."

CHAPTER III.
THE OLD SCHOOLMASTER'S FIDDLE.

Stineli and Rico freed themselves from the crowd of children gathered before the schoolhouse, and wandered off together. "Were you thinking so that you could not sing with us to-day, Rico?" asked Stineli. "Were you thinking again about the lake?"

"No, it was quite another thing," replied the boy. "I know how to play 'Little lambkins, come down,' if I only had a fiddle."

Judging from the deep sigh that accompanied these words, the wish must have weighed heavily on Rico's heart. The sympathetic little Stineli began at once to contrive some means of helping him to get his wish.

"We will buy one together, Rico," she said suddenly, full of delight at a happy thought that had entered her head. I have ever so many pieces of money,--as many as twelve. How much have you got?"

"None at all," said the boy sadly. "My father gave me some before he went away, but my cousin said I should only spend it foolishly, and she took it from me, and put it up on the shelf in a box where I cannot get it."

Such a trifle did not discourage Stineli. "Perhaps we have enough without that, and my grandmother will give me some more soon," she said consolingly. "You know, Rico, a fiddle can't cost so very much; it is nothing but a bit of old wood with four strings stretched across it, that will be cheap, I'm sure. You must ask the teacher about it to-morrow morning, and then we will try to find one."

So it was settled, and Stineli resolved to do all she could at home to make herself useful by getting up bright and early, and making the fire before her mother was afoot, thinking that, if she worked busily from morning till night, perhaps her grandmother would put a bit of money for her in the bag.

After school the next day Stineli went out and waited alone behind the wood-pile at the schoolhouse corner, for Rico had made up his mind at last to ask the teacher how much it would cost to buy a fiddle. He was such a long time about it, that Stineli kept peeping out from behind the wood-pile, quite overcome with impatience, but only saw the other school children who were standing about and playing; but now certainly,--yes, that was Rico who came around the corner.

"What did he say? How much does it cost?" cried Stineli, almost breathless with suspense.

"I had not the courage to ask," was the sad answer.

"Oh, what a shame!" said the girl, and stood still and disappointed for a moment, but not more. "Never mind, Rico; you can try again to-morrow," she said cheerfully, taking him by the hand and turning homeward. "I got another bit of money from my grandmother this morning, because I got up early and was in the kitchen when she came in."

The same thing happened, however, the next day and the day after. Rico stood for half an hour before the door without getting courage to go in to ask his question. At last Stineli made up her mind to go herself, if this lasted three days more. On the fourth day, however, as Rico was standing, timid and depressed, before the door, it opened suddenly, and the teacher came out quickly, and ran into Rico with such force, that the slender little fellow, who did not weigh more than a feather, was thrown backward several feet. The teacher stood looking at the child in great surprise and some displeasure. Then he said, "What does this mean, Rico? Why do you stand before the door without knocking, if you have a message to deliver? If you have no message, why do you not go away? If you wish to tell me any thing, do so at once. What is it that you wish?"

"How much does a fiddle cost?" Rico blurted out his question in great fear and haste. The teacher's surprise and displeasure increased visibly.

"I do not understand, Rico," he said, with a severe glance at the boy. Have you come here on purpose to mock me? or have you any particular reason for asking this? What did you mean to say?"

"I did not mean any thing," said Rico abashed, "only to ask how much it would cost to buy a fiddle."

"You did not understand me just now,--pay attention to what I am saying. There are two ways of asking a question: either to obtain information, or simply from idle curiosity, which is foolishness. Now pay attention, Rico: is this a mere idle question, or did somebody send you who wishes to buy a fiddle?"

"I want to buy one myself," said the boy, taking courage a little; but he was frightened when the angry reply came, "What! what did you say? A forlorn little fellow like you buy a fiddle! Do you even know what the instrument is? Have you any idea of how old I was, and what I knew, before I obtained one? I was a teacher, a regular teacher; was twenty-two years old, with an assured profession, and not a child like you.

"Now I will tell you what a fiddle costs, and then you will see how foolish you are. Six hard gulden I paid for mine. Can you realize what that means? We will separate it into blutsgers. If one gulden contains a hundred blutsgers, then six guldens will be equal to six times one hundred,--quickly, quickly! Now, Rico, you are generally ready enough."

"Six hundred blutsgers," said the lad softly, for he was quite overpowered with the magnitude of this sum as compared with Stineli's twelve blutsgers.

"And, moreover, my son, do you imagine that you have only to take a fiddle in your hand to be able to play on it at once? It takes a long time to do that. Come in here now, for a moment." And the teacher opened the door, and took his fiddle from its place on the wall. "There," he said, as he placed it on Rico's arm, "take the bow in your hand,--so, my boy; and if you can play me *c, d, e, f,* I will give you a half-gulden."

Rico had the fiddle really in his hand; his eyes sparkled with fire; *c, d, e, f,*--he played the notes firmly and perfectly correctly. "You little rascal!" cried the astonished teacher, "where did you learn that? Who taught you? How do you find the notes?"

"I can do more than that, if I may," said the boy.

"Play, then."

And Rico played correctly, and with enthusiasm,--

"Little lambkins, come down From the bright sunny height;　　　　The day-light is fading, The sun says, 'Good-night!'"

The teacher sunk into a chair, and put his spectacles on his nose. His eyes rested on Rico's fingers as he played, then on his sparkling eyes, and again on his hands. When the air was finished, he said, "Come here to me, Rico;" and, moving his chair into the light, he placed the lad directly before him. "Now I have something to say to you. Your father is an Italian; and I know that down there all sorts of things go on of which we have no idea here in the mountains. Now look me straight in the eye, and answer me truly and honestly. How did you learn to play this air so correctly?"

Looking up with his honest eyes, the boy replied, "I learned it from you, in the school where it is so often sung."

These words gave an entirely new aspect to the affair. The teacher stood up, and went back and forth several times in the room. Then he was himself the cause of this wonderful event; there was no necromancy concerned in it.

In a far better humor, he took out his purse, saying, "Here is your half-gulden, Rico; it is justly yours. Now go; and for the future be very attentive to the music-lesson as long as you go to the school. In that way you may, perhaps, accomplish something; and in twelve or fourteen years perhaps you may be able to buy a fiddle. Now you may go."

Rico cast one look at the fiddle, and departed with deep sadness in his heart.

Stineli came running to meet him from behind the wood-pile. "You did stay a long time. Have you asked the question?"

"It is all of no use," said the boy; and his eyebrows came together in his distress, and formed a thick black line across his forehead over his eyes. "A fiddle costs six hundred blutsgers; and in fourteen years I can buy one, when everybody will be dead. Who will be living fourteen years from now? There, you may have this; I do not want it." With these words he pressed the half-gulden into Stineli's hand.

"Six hundred blutsgers!" repeated the girl, horrified. "But where did this half-gulden come from?"

Rico told her all that had happened at the teacher's, ending with the same words expressing his great regret, "It is all of no use!"

Stineli tried to console him a little with the half-gulden; but he was furious at the thought of the innocent piece of money, and would not even look at it.

So Stineli said, "I will put it with my blutsgers, and we will have it all between us."

Stineli herself was very much discouraged now; but as they went around the corner into the field, the little pathway that led to their doors shone so prettily in the bright sunlight, and the plat before the houses was so white and dry, that she called out,--

"See, see! now it is summer, Rico; and we can go up into the wood, and we will be happy again. Shall we go next Sunday?"

"Nothing will ever make me happy again," said Rico; "but if you want to go, I will go with you."

When they reached the door, they had arranged to go to the wood on the following Sunday, and Stineli was very happy at the thought. She did all that she was able to do through the week, and there was a great deal of work for her. Peterli, Sami, and Urschli had the measles, and in the stable one of the goats was sick, and needed hot water very often; and Stineli had to run hither and thither, lending a helping hand in every direction as soon as she came home from school, and on Saturday all day long until late in the evening; and then there were the stable buckets to be cleaned. But that night her father said,--

"Stineli *is* a handy child."

CHAPTER IV.
THE BEAUTIFUL DISTANT LAKE
WITHOUT A NAME

When Stineli awoke on the following Sunday morning, she was conscious of an unusual light-heartedness, and at first could not understand the cause, until she remembered what day it was, and that her grandmother had said, on the previous evening, "To-morrow you must have the whole afternoon to yourself: it is rightfully yours."

After dinner was finished, and all the dishes taken away, and the table washed off by Stineli, Peterli called out, "Come here to me;" and the two others screamed, "No, to me!" and her father said, "Now Stineli must go to look after the goats."

But at this moment her grandmother went through the kitchen, and made a sign to Stineli to follow her.

"Now go in peace, my child," she said. "I will take care of the goats and the children; but be sure to come home, both of you, punctually when the bell rings for prayer." The grandmother knew very well that there were two of them.

Off flew Stineli, like a bird whose cage-door has suddenly been opened; and outside stood Rico, who had been waiting for a long time. They went on together, across the meadow towards the wood.

On the mountains the sun was shining brightly, and the blue heavens lay over all the landscape. They were obliged to pass, for a little while, through the shade in the snow; but the sun was shining a little farther on, and shimmered on the waters of the lake, and there were lovely dry spots on the slope that was almost hanging over the lake.

There the children seated themselves. A sharp wind came down from the heights, and whistled about their ears. Stineli was as happy as happy could be. She shouted out, again and again, "Oh, look, Rico; look! How beautiful it is in the sun! Now summer has come, look how the lake glistens! There cannot be a more beautiful lake than this one anywhere," she said confidently.

"Yes, yes, Stineli! You ought to see the lake I know about just once," said Rico; and looked so longingly across the lake, that it seemed as if that which he wanted to see began just beyond their vision.

"Over there are no dark fir-trees, with sharp needles, but shining green leaves, and great red flowers; and the mountains are not so high and dark, nor so near, but lie off in the distance, and are purple; and the sky and the lake are all golden and still and warm. There the wind does not feel like this, and one's feet never get full of snow; and one can sit all day long on the sunny ground, and look about."

Stineli was quite carried away by this description. She already saw the red flowers and the golden lake before her eyes, and seemed to know exactly how beautiful it all was.

"Perhaps you may be able to go there again to see it all, Rico. Do you know the way?"

"You must cross the Maloja. I have been there with my father once. He pointed me out the road that goes all the way down the mountain,--first this way, then that. and far below lies the lake; but so far, so far, that it is scarcely possible to go there."

"Oh! that is easy enough," said Stineli. "You have to go farther and farther, that is all; and at the end you will surely get there."

"But my father told me something else. Do you know, Stineli, when you are travelling and stop at an inn, and eat something and sleep there, then there is something to pay, and you must have money for that."

"Oh! we have lots of money," cried Stineli triumphantly. But her companion was not triumphant.

"That is exactly as good as nothing. I know that by the affair of the fiddle," he said sadly.

"Then it will be better for you to stay at home, Rico. Look! it is beautiful here at home, I am sure."

The lad sat thoughtfully silent for a long time, leaning his head on his hand, and his eyebrows brought in a close line down over his eyes. At last he turned again to Stineli, who had been gathering the soft green moss that grew around the spot where they were lying, and of which she made a tiny bed with two pillows and a coverlet. She meant to carry them home to the sick Urschli.

"You say I had better stay at home, Stineli; but, do you know, it is just as if I did not know where my home really is."

"Oh, dear me! what do you mean?" cried the girl; and in her surprise she threw away a whole handful of moss. Your home is here, of course. It is always home where father and mother"--She stopped suddenly. Rico had no mother, and his father had been away now for a very long time; and the cousin? Stineli never went near that cousin, who had never spoken one pleasant word to her. The child did not know what to say, but it was not natural to her to remain long in uncertainty. Rico had already fallen into one of his reveries, when she grasped him by the arm, and said,--

"I should just like to know something; that is, the name of the lake where it is so lovely."

Rico pondered. "I do not know," he said; and felt very much surprised himself as he spoke.

Now Stineli proposed that they should ask somebody what it was called; for even if Rico had ever so much money, and was able to travel, he must know how to inquire the way, and what the name of the lake was. They began at once to think of whom they should inquire,--of the teacher, or of the grandmother.

At last it occurred to Rico that his father would know better than anybody else, and he thought he would certainly ask him when he came home again.

The time had slipped away quickly as they sat talking, and presently the children heard the distant sound of a bell. They recognized the sound. It was the bell for prayers.

They sprang up quickly, and ran off, hand in hand, down the hill-side through bushes, and through the snow across the meadow; and it had scarcely stopped ringing when they reached the door where the grandmother was on the lookout for them.

Stineli had to go at once into the house, and her grandmother said quickly, "Go home directly, Rico, and do not hang around the door any longer."

The grandmother had never said such a thing to him before, although he had always been in the habit of hanging around the door; for he was never in haste to go home, and stood always for a while before he could make up his mind to enter. He obeyed at once, however, and went into the house.

CHAPTER V.
A SAD HOUSE, BUT THE LAKE GETS A NAME.

Rico did not find his cousin in the sitting-room; so he went to the kitchen, and opened the door. There she stood; but before he could enter, she raised her finger, saying, "Sch! sch! Do not open and shut the doors, and make a noise, as if there were four of you. Go into the other room, and keep still. Your father is lying in the bedroom up there. They brought him home in a wagon: he is sick."

Rico went into the room, seated himself on a bench, and did not stir.

He sat there for at least a half-hour. Presently he heard the cousin moving about in the kitchen. Then he thought that he would go up very softly, and peep into the bedroom. Perhaps his father would like something to eat: it was long past the meal-time.

He slipped behind the stove, mounted the little steps, and went very softly into the bedroom. After a while he returned, went at once into the kitchen, approached quite close to his cousin, and said softly,--

"Cousin, come up."

The woman was about to strike him angrily, when she happened to glance at his face. He was perfectly colorless,--cheeks and lips as white as a sheet, and his eyes looked so black that the cousin was almost afraid of him.

"What is the matter with you?" she asked hastily, and followed him almost involuntarily.

He mounted the little steps softly, and entered the chamber. His father lay on the bed with staring, wide-open eyes,--he was dead.

"Oh, my God!" screamed the cousin, and ran crying out of the door that opened upon the passage on the other side of the room, went down the staircase, and across into the opposite house, where she called out to tell the neighbor and the grand-mother the sad news; and thence she ran on to the teacher and to the mayor.

One after another they came, and entered the quiet room until it was full of people; for the news spread from one to another of what had taken place. And in the midst of all the tumult, and of all the clamor of the crowd of neighbors, Rico stood by the bedside speechless, motionless, and gazed at his father. All through the week the house was filled with people who wished to look at the man, and hear from the cousin how it had all happened; so that the lad heard it repeated over and over, that his father had been at work down in St. Gall on the railroad.

He had received a deep wound on the head when they were blasting a rock; and, as he could not work any longer, he wished to go home to take care of himself until the wound was healed. But the long journey--sometimes on foot, sometimes in an open wagon--was too much for him; and when he had reached his home on Sunday, towards evening, he he had lain down on the bed never to rise again. Without any one knowing it, he had passed away; for he was already stiff when

Rico had found him. On the following Sunday the burial took place. Rico was the only mourner to follow the coffin. Several kind neighbors joined in, and thus the little procession went on to Sils. In the church, Rico heard the pastor when he read out, "The deceased was called Henrico Trevillo, and was a native of Peschiera on the Lake of Garda."

These words brought the feeling to Rico that he had heard something that he knew perfectly well before, and yet could not recollect. He had always seen a picture of the lake before his eyes when he had sung,--

"One evening   In Peschiera,"

with his father, but he had never known the reason. He repeated the name softly to himself, while one old song after another arose in his memory.

As he came back from the burial all alone, he saw the grandmother seated on the log of wood, and Stineli by her side. She beckoned him to come over to them. She gave the lad a bit of cake and another to Stineli, and said now they might go off together for a walk. Rico ought not to be alone.

So the children rambled off together, hand in hand. The grandmother remained seated on her log, sadly gazing after the black-haired lad until they had wandered slowly up the hillside and passed out of sight. Then she said softly to herself,--

"Whate'er He does, or lets be done,
  Is always for the best."

CHAPTER VI.
RICO'S MOTHER.

Along the road from Sils came the teacher leaning on his staff. He had assisted at the burial. He coughed and cleared his throat; and as he drew near to the grandmother and bade her "good evening," he seated himself by her side. "If you have no objection, I will sit here with you for a few moments, neighbor," said he; "for I feel very badly in my throat and chest. But what can we expect when we are almost seventy years old, and have witnessed such a funeral as this one to-day? He was not thirty-five years of age, and as strong as a tree."

"It always sets me thinking," said the grandmother, "when I, an old woman of seventy-five years, am left, and here and there a young person is called away,--a useful one, too."

"Yet the old folks are good for something. Who else can set an example to the youth?" remarked the teacher. "But what is your opinion, neighbor: what will become of the little fellow over yonder, do you think?"

"Yes, what will become of him?" repeated the old woman. "I also ask myself that question; and if my only reliance were upon human help, I should not know of an answer. But there is a heavenly Father who looks after the forsaken children. He will provide something for the lad."

"Will you not tell me, neighbor, how it happened that the Italian married the daughter of your friend who lived over there opposite? One never knows how these people may turn out."

"It happened as such things always happen, neighbor. You know how my old friend Anne-Dete had lost all her children, and her husband also, and lived alone in the cottage over yonder with Marie-Seppli, who was a merry little girl. About eleven or twelve years ago Trevillo made his appearance here. He had work in the Maloja, and came down here with the other boys; and he and Marie-Seppli had scarcely become acquainted before they were resolved to have each other.

"And it must be said, in justice to Trevillo, that he was not only a handsome fellow who was agreeable to everybody, but also an industrious and well-conducted man, with whom Anne-Dete (the mother) was well pleased. Naturally she wished that they should stay in the house and live with her, and Trevillo would gladly have done so. He was fond of his wife's mother, and he always did as Marie-Seppli wished him to. He had taken her, however, towards the Maloja in his walks, and they had together looked down the road where you can see how far it goes winding down the mountain; and he had told her how every thing was down there where he was born. So Marie-Seppli got it into her head that she must go there, and no matter how much her mother worried and fretted, and said that they could not live there, she still was bent upon going; and Trevillo himself said that as to living there she need not fear, for he had a nice little property and a house; but, for his part, he would like to see a little of the world. But the bride prevailed, and after the wedding she was all for starting directly down the mountain.

"She wrote to her mother occasionally that it was very nice where they lived, and that Trevillo was the best of husbands.

"About five or six years later, who should walk into the room where Anne-Dete was sitting but Trevillo, leading a little boy by the hand. He said, 'There, mother, this is the only thing I have left of Marie-Seppli. She lies buried down yonder with her other little children. This one was her first, and her favorite.'

"This is what my old friend told me. Then he threw himself down on the bench where he had first seen his wife, saying that he should like to make his home there with her and the boy, if she had no objection, for down below it was not possible for him to continue to live. This was joy and sorrow at the same time for Anne-Dete.

"Little Rico was then about four years old,--a quiet, thoughtful boy, never noisy or mischievous, and the very apple of her eye; but she died in the course of a year, and Trevillo was advised to take a cousin of hers to keep house for him and his boy."

"So, so!" said the teacher when the old woman was silent, having finished her story. "I had not understood all this thoroughly before. Perhaps some of Trevillo's relations will come forward, in good time, and they can be asked to do something for the child."

"Relations!" said the grandmother with a sigh. "That cousin is a relation, and little enough of comfort he gets from her in the course of the year."

The schoolmaster rose with difficulty from his seat. "I am going down-hill, neighbor," he said, shaking his head. "I cannot imagine where my strength has gone to."

The old woman encouraged him, and said he was still a young man in comparison with her. But, in truth, it did surprise her to see how slowly and painfully he walked as he left her.

CHAPTER VII.
A PRECIOUS LEGACY, AND A PRECIOUS PRAYER.

Many beautiful Sundays followed; and, whenever it was possible, the grandmother so arranged it that Stineli got, now and then, a spare moment; but the work in the house increased daily. Rico passed many hours standing on the threshold of his cottage looking longingly across the way, in the hope of seeing Stineli come out.

Towards September, when people often sat before their houses in order to enjoy, to the utmost, the last warm evenings of the season, the schoolmaster placed himself before his door, but he looked very thin and coughed continually; and at last, one morning when he tried to rise, his strength deserted him completely, and he fell back upon his pillow.

There he lay very still, and busy with all sorts of thoughts; and he wondered what would come to pass when he died. He had no children, and his wife had been dead for a long time, and there was only in old maid-servant to live with him and take care of the house. He was principally occupied in thinking of what would become of all the things that belonged to him when he should be gone; and, as his fiddle hung directly opposite to him on the wall, he said to himself, "I must leave that behind me too."

Then he remembered the day when Rico stood before him and played on the instrument, and he felt as if he had rather let the boy have the fiddle than to let it go to a distant cousin who did not understand the use of it at all. And he thought that, if it were to go very cheap, perhaps Rico could buy it. Presently he bethought himself that if he could not use the violin, neither would he have any use for money. For all that, he could not bring himself to let the instrument, for which he had paid down six hard gulden, go for nothing.

So he pondered and pondered how he could manage to obtain something in exchange; but at last it was quite clear to him that there, where he was fast going, he could not take his violin with him, neither could he take any thing that he might get for it, for all must remain behind.

While he was lying there the fever became greater and greater, and he lay, towards evening and all night long, fighting with all sorts of strange thoughts, and old, long-forgotten events rose before his mind and perplexed him; so that at last, towards morning, he lay on his bed utterly exhausted, and with only one thought or wish,--viz., to be able to do one kind deed, one good action, and that quickly, before it was too late. He knocked against the wall with his stick until the old maid-servant heard him and came in to him; and then he sent her over to the grandmother, to ask her to come to him as quickly as possible.

She did come almost immediately; and before she had fairly time to ask him how he found himself, he said,--

"Will you be so good as to take down the fiddle that hangs there on the wall, and give it to the little orphan boy? I wish to make him a present of it, and he must be very careful of it."

Naturally the good woman was very much surprised, and could not refrain from exclaiming repeatedly, "What will Rico do with it? What will Rico say to this?" Presently she noticed, however, that the schoolmaster seemed a little restless, as if he were in a hurry to have the thing done.

So she left him, and hastened as quickly as possible across the fields with the gift under her arm; for she was also impatient to know how Rico would take this rare piece of good fortune.

He was standing in the doorway of his cottage. At a motion from the grandmother, he ran towards her.

"Here, Rico," she said, and handed him the violin. "The schoolmaster sends this to you: it is yours."

The boy stood as if he were in a dream, but it was true. The grandmother was really standing there, holding the fiddle out to him.

Trembling with pleasure and excitement, he took his present at last, put it on his arm, and gazed at it in a silly sort of way, as if he thought it might vanish presently, as quickly as it had come, if he did not keep his eyes on it.

"You must be very careful of it," said the old woman, delivering her message faithfully. She was much inclined to laugh, however; for it did not seem to her that the warning was at all necessary. "And, Rico, think about the teacher, and do not forget what he has done for you: he is very ill."

The grandmother went into the house with these words; and the boy hastened up into his own bedroom, where he was always alone.

There he sat and fiddled, and played on and on, and forgot all about eating or drinking, or how the time sped on. At last, when it was almost dark, he came to himself, and went down-stairs. The cousin came out from the kitchen, saying, "You can have something to eat to-morrow morning. You have behaved so to-day that you won't get any thing more."

The boy did not feel hungry, although he had not eaten since the early morning, and went quite unconsciously across into the opposite house, and entered the kitchen. He was looking for the grandmother.

Stineli was standing by the hearth, arranging the fire. When she caught sight of Rico, she shouted aloud for joy; for the ground had almost burned beneath her feet, she had been so impatient all day--ever since her grandmother had told her the great news--to get away, and express her delight to Rico; but she had not dared to leave the house for an instant. Now she was fairly beside herself, and called out, again and again, "You have got it now! You have got it now!"

Hearing the noise, the grandmother came out of the sitting-room; and Rico hastened towards her, saying, "May I go to thank the teacher, if he is sick?"

After thinking a while,--for she remembered how very ill the schoolmaster looked in the morning when she saw him,--the good woman said, "Wait a few moments, Rico, I will go with you;" and stepped into her room to put on a clean apron. Then they went over to the schoolhouse. The grandmother entered first. Rico followed, his fiddle under his arm. He had not once laid it down since it had come into his possession.

The teacher lay on his bed, looking very feeble indeed. The lad stepped to the bedside and looked down at his fiddle and could scarcely speak, but his eyes sparkled so brightly that the good man had no difficulty in understanding him: he cast a pleased look towards the boy, and nodded at him. Then he beckoned the grandmother to draw near. Rico moved a little to one side, and the teacher said with a weak voice, "Grandmother, I should be very glad if you would say 'Our Father' for me, I feel so very much troubled."

Just at this moment the prayer-bell sounded. The grandmother folded her hands and repeated the Lord's Prayer, and Rico also folded his hands. Every thing was quiet in the room. After a while the grandmother bent over and closed the old teacher's eyes, for he had passed away. Then she took Rico by the hand, and went softly home with him.

CHAPTER VIII.
ON THE LAKE OF SILS.

Stineli did not recover herself during the entire week, her joy was so great; but it seemed as if that week were ten days longer than any other, for Sunday seemed never to come.

At last it did come, and a golden sun shone over the harvest fields, and she and Rico went up under the fir-trees, where the sparkling lake lay spread out at their feet; and the girl's heart was so overflowing with happiness, that she had to dance about and shout aloud before she seated herself on the moss, on the very edge of the slope. There she could see every thing round about,--the sunny heights and the lake, and, stretched over all, the blue heavens.

Suddenly she called out, "Come now, Rico; we will sing,--sing for ever so long."

So the lad seated himself by Stineli's side, and placed his fiddle in position,--for he had, of course, brought that too,--and began to play, and the children sang,--

"Little lambkins, come down From the bright, sunny height,"
until they had sung all the verses; but Stineli had not had half enough.
"We will sing more," she said, and went on,--

"Little lambkins, above
On the bright, pleasant hill,
The sunlight is sparkling,
The winds are not still."
And then Rico sang the verse and was pleased and said, "Sing some more."
Stineli was quite excited: thought a bit, and looked up, then down, and sang again,--
"And the lambkins, and the lambkins,
And the heavens so blue;
And red and white flowers,
And the green grasses, too."

Then Rico fiddled and sung the verse with her, and said again, "Some more."
Stineli laughed, and, glancing at Rico, sang,--
  "And a sad little boy,
And a very gay maid;
And a lake like another,
That from water is made."
Laughing and singing, Stineli went on,--
  "And the lambkins, and the lambkins,
They jumped up so high,
And all were most merry,
And did not know why.
  "And a boy and a girl
By the lake-side did sit,
And because they forgot it,
It hurt not a bit."

Now they began at the very beginning, and sang the whole thing through again, and made merry over it, and were so happy that they sang it at least ten times over; and the more they repeated it, the better it sounded to their ears.

After this Rico played several tunes that he had learned from his father; but they soon came back to their own song, and began that again.

In the midst of it the girl stopped and said, "It has just come into my head how you can go down to the other lake, and will not need any money either."

Rico paused suddenly and gazed at his companion, awaiting what was coming next.

"Don't you see," she said earnestly, "now you have a fiddle, and you know a song. You can go and play your song, and sing before the taverns; then the people will give you something to eat and to drink, and let you sleep there, for they will see that you are not a beggar. So you can go on until you reach the lake; and, coming home, you can do the same thing again."

Rico reflected over these words, but Stineli would give him no time for dreaming: she wanted to go on with the song.

They made so much noise themselves, that they did not hear the prayer-bell at all; and did not notice what time it was until reminded by the growing darkness, and perceived the grandmother looking about anxiously for them before they reached the houses.

But Stineli was too much excited to be subdued by any thing. She ran on towards her grandmother, and said, "You have no idea how beautifully Rico can fiddle; and we have made a song of our own, for ourselves only. We will sing it to you this very moment."

And before there was time to answer, they began and sang it all through; and the good grandmother listened with real pleasure to their sweet, clear voices.

She seated herself on the log; and, when the children had finished, said, "Come now, Rico, I want you to play for me; and you and I will sing together. Do you know the song that begins,--

"'I sing to thee with heart and voice?'"

Rico had probably heard the hymn, but he did not know it correctly, and said that he wished first to hear it from the grandmother, and he would follow her softly on his violin, and then he would be sure of it.

So they began; and first the grandmother repeated the words of a verse to the children, and then they all sang it together,--

"I sing to thee with heart and voice,
Lord, whom my soul obeys.
I sing, and bid all earth rejoice:
Thou teachest me thy praise.
    "I know that thou the fountain art
Of joy,--the eternal spring
Which, into every willing heart,
Healing and good dost bring.
    "Why do we worry over sin?
Why sorrow night and day?
Come, bring thy load, cast it on Him
Who fashioned thee from clay.
    "He never yet has done amiss;
And, perfect in His sight,

All that He does or orders is
Sure to be finished right.
  "Now only let His will be done,
Nor clamor constantly,
Peace to thy heart on earth will come,
And joy eternally."

"It is well," said the grandmother. "Now we know a proper evening hymn, and you may go quickly to rest, my children."

CHAPTER IX.
A PERPLEXING AFFAIR.

When Rico entered the cottage that evening it was later than usual, for he had spent a full half-hour in singing the hymn. As he went in, his cousin came flying towards him.

"Are you beginning in this style already?" she called out. "The supper stood waiting for you a whole hour: now I have put it away. Go to your bedroom: and if you turn out a good-for-nothing and a scamp, it is no fault of mine. I don't know any thing that I had not rather do than look after a boy like you."

Rico never answered a single word, no matter how much his cousin might scold at him; but this evening he looked at her, and said,--

"I can get out of your way, cousin."

She shoved the bolt in on the house-door with such violence that the door shook, and went into the sitting-room, slamming that door behind her. Rico went up into his dark little bedroom.

On the following day, as all the big family in the other cottage were eating their supper,--the parents, the grandmother, and all the children,--the cousin came running over, and called out from the door to ask if they knew any thing about Rico: she had no idea where he could be.

"He will come fast enough when it is time for supper," replied the father quietly.

The cousin entered the room. She had been quite sure that the lad was there, and she expected him to come out if she only stood at the door and asked for him.

Now she went on to tell them that he had not made his appearance at breakfast, nor at dinner-time, and that he had not been in bed the previous night, for she had found it as she had left it; and she believed that he must have gone away very early in the morning before daybreak, wandering about as he was in the habit of doing, for the bolt was pushed aside on the house-door when she went to open it. She thought at first that she must have forgotten to bolt it the night before in her anger, for nobody knew how angry she had been.

"Something has happened to him," said the father, quite unmoved. "He has probably fallen into some cleft up there on the mountain: it often happens to little boys who go climbing about everywhere.

"You ought to have spoken of it earlier in the day," he went on slowly. "We shall have to go to look for him, and in the night you can't see any thing."

At these words the cousin broke out into a terrible uproar. She expected there would be all sorts of fault found with her; that was always the way when you had suffered for years, and never said any thing about it.

"Nobody would ever believe," she said,--and spoke a truthful word then, at least,--"what a sly, cunning, deceitful boy that is, and what a life he has led me these four years. He will turn out a regular vagabond, a tramp, a disgraceful creature."

The grandmother had ceased eating for several minutes. She now rose from the table, and went up to the cousin, who was talking very noisily.

"Stop, neighbor, stop," she said; and repeated it twice without effect. "I know Rico very well; I have always known him ever since he was brought here to his grandmother. If I were in your place, I would not say another word, but stop to think whether the lad, to whom perhaps something dreadful has happened, and who may be standing up there before God at this moment, may not have some complaint against somebody,--somebody who had done him a heavy injury, all deserted as he is, with her cruel words."

Since Rico's disappearance, the way the lad looked at her on that last evening had occurred several times to the cousin's mind, and how he said,--

"I can easily get out of your way."

That was why she had made such a noise about it, in order to drown these words. Now she did not dare to look the grandmother in the face, but said that she must go: perhaps Rico might be at the cottage by this time, which she would very gladly have had come true.

From this day forward the cousin never spoke another word against Rico in the grandmother's hearing; nor, indeed, did she often speak of him at all. She believed, as did all the neighbors far and near, that the lad was dead; and she was thankful that nobody knew about the words he had said to her on that last evening.

The next morning after this event was made known, Stineli's father went out to the thrashing-floor and picked himself out a stout stick. He said that he would call some of the neighbors together: they must go search for the lad somewhere towards the glaciers and up by the ravines.

Stineli crept out after him, and he said, when he noticed her, "That is right, come and help me to search; you can get into the corners better than I can."

At last, after they had found a big beanpole, Stineli ventured to say, "But father, if Rico went along the high-road, then he could not fall into any thing, could he?"

"Oh, perhaps he might," replied her father. "Such thoughtless boys as he often stray off the road, and fall into ravines and places: they don't know themselves where they are going, and he was always moving about more or less."

That this was true of Rico nobody knew better than Stineli; and she became dreadfully anxious from that time forth, which anxiety increased every day to such a degree that she could neither eat nor sleep for sorrow, and did her work, day after day, as if she did not know what she was about.

Rico was not found: nobody had seen any thing of him. They ceased to search for him, and the folks soon began to find consolation in the thought, "It is just as well for the little fellow, after all; he was forsaken, and had no one to care for him."

CHAPTER X.
A LITTLE LIGHT.

Stineli grew more and more thin and quiet from day to day. The little ones called out complainingly, "Stineli never tells us stories now, and never laughs any more." Her mother said to her father, "Do you notice how changed she is?" And her father replied, "It is because she grows so fast. She must get a little goat's milk early in the mornings."

After this had gone on for three weeks or so, Stineli's grandmother called the girl into her bedroom one evening, and said, "My dear Stineli, I can very well understand that you cannot forget your friend Rico, but you must try to remember that it is God's will that he should be taken away; and that, as it is so, it is also the best thing for Rico, as we must try to think."

At these words Stineli began to weep as her grandmother had never seen her do before; and she sobbed and sobbed, saying, "The good God did not do it: I did it, grandmother; and therefore I feel as if I should die of anxiety. It was I who proposed to Rico to go to find the lake, and now he has fallen into a ravine, and is dead; it has hurt him dreadfully, and it is all my fault." Then the poor child cried and sobbed pitifully. It seemed to the grandmother as if a heavy weight were lifted from her heart as she heard these words of Stineli's. She had given up Rico as lost; and had in secret believed that the child had fled from the unkind treatment he had received at home, and was lying somewhere in the water, or was lost in the woods. Now a new hope arose in her heart.

She succeeded in quieting Stineli enough to persuade her to relate the whole story about the lake, of which the grandmother was in total ignorance: how Rico had always been talking about this lake, and how he had longed to go to find it, and how, at last, Stineli had suggested the way for him to do so. It really seemed most likely that Rico had started to find the lake, but her father's mention of the ravines had destroyed all hope in Stineli.

The good old woman took her granddaughter by the hand, and drew her towards her, saying, "Now, Stineli, I have something to explain to you. Do you remember what the old song says,--the one we sang with Rico on the last evening we were together?--

"'All that He does or orders is Sure to be finished right.'"

Now you see, that although the good God did not exactly do this thing,--as if He had let Rico die in his bed, for instance,--yet the thing is in His hand all the same, although you have it turned aside, perhaps, a little; for certainly the good God is stronger than this little Stineli. And, now that you have made this sad mistake, it will be a lesson to you for all the rest of your life, no matter how it may turn out in the end, that children should not run away into the unknown world, nor undertake things about which they are utterly ignorant; and that without saying a word to their parents or to their grandmothers, who love them so well. But now the kind God has allowed it to happen, and we may certainly hope that it will all be finished right.

"Now ponder this well, my Stineli, and never forget what you have thus learned by experience; and now--for I see how heavily it weighs down your heart--it will be well for you to go to pray to the good God, that He will allow this mistake of yours and Rico to turn out all right. And then you can be happy again, Stineli, and I shall be so, too; for I believe firmly that Rico is living, and that the good God has not forsaken him."

And Stineli became after this like her former happy self; and, although she missed Rico constantly, still she no longer felt worried, nor did she reproach herself, but looked continually down the road to Maloja, expecting to see him.

CHAPTER XI.
A LONG JOURNEY.

On that memorable Sunday evening, Rico seated himself on the chair in his gloomy bedroom. There he decided to stay until his cousin had gone to bed.

After Stineli had made the discovery that Rico could go with his fiddle down to the much-wished-for lake, the enterprise seemed a very simple thing to the lad,--so easy, that he only thought of the best way to get off. He had a presentiment that his cousin would probably try to hinder him from going, although he felt sure that she would not miss him after he was away.

So, when she began to scold him when he came home, he said to himself, "I will be off as soon as she is once in her bed."

He had very pleasant thoughts as he sat there in the dark,--of how nice it would be not to hear the scolding voice of his cousin all day long, and of what big bushels of the red flowers he would bring back to Stineli when he returned. And then the picture of the sunny shores of the lake and the purple hills rose before his mind, and he fell asleep. He was not in a very comfortable position, for he had never let his fiddle leave his hand; and he soon awoke again, but it was still dark.

Now he had a clear idea of what he would do. He had his Sunday clothes on, which was good; and his cap was also on his head. He took his fiddle under his arm, and went softly down the steps, slipped the bolt aside, and stole out into the cool air of morning.

The dawn was just showing over the mountains, and in Sils the cocks were crowing. Off he walked briskly, to get well away from the houses and to reach the highway. When he once was on the road, he went along merrily; for he felt quite at home there, he had so often traversed the ground with his father. He could form no idea of how far it really was to the Maloja; and indeed it seemed very long to him, after he had been going for two good hours. Little by little it grew brighter, however; and in about an hour more, when he reached the place before the tavern upon the Maloja, where he used to stand with his father and gaze down the mountain road, the sunny light of morning lay upon the mountains, and the tips of the fir-trees were all touched with gold.

Rico seated himself upon the edge of the roadside. He was very tired, and remembered suddenly that he had not eaten any thing since the noonday meal of the day before. But he was not discouraged, for now the way was all down hill; and, after that, he should undoubtedly reach the lake.

While he sat there, the big post-wagon came rumbling along. He had often seen it as it came through Sils, and always thought that the very greatest happiness upon earth must be experienced by the driver, who sat all day long on the box, and controlled his four horses with his whip. Now he saw this happy creature nearer; for the post-wagon stopped, and the lad never once removed his eyes from the wonderful man, as he came down from his perch, stepped into the inn, and came out again with an enormous piece of black bread in his hand, upon which lay a large piece of cheese.

Next, the driver drew out a strong knife, cut a good big bit of bread, and gave each horse a mouthful in turn, not forgetting himself in the meantime; but upon his own piece of bread he put an equally big morsel of cheese. As they all stood there, eating in happy companionship, the man looked about a little, and presently called out, "Hulloa, little musician! won't you join us too? Come hither."

Now when Rico saw them all eating, he fully realized how very hungry he was. He most gladly accepted the invitation, and approached the driver, who cut such a big slice of bread and also of cheese to give the lad, that Rico did not really know how he should manage to eat it.

He was obliged to put his fiddle down on the ground; and the coachman looked on very complaisantly while the boy ate his breakfast, and said, while he followed his own occupation,--

"You are a very small fiddler. Do you know how to play something?"

"Oh, yes! two songs, besides those I learned from my father," replied Rico.

"Really! And where are you going to on your two little legs?" said the driver. "To Peschiera, on the Lake of Garda," was the serious answer.

At these words, the coachman burst into such boisterous laughter that the boy gazed up at him in great astonishment.

"Well, you are a good one to travel," cried the man, still laughing." Have you any notion how far it is, and that a little musician like you could wear out his two feet, and his soles, too, before he could catch sight of a single drop of the water of the Lake of Garda? Who sends you down there?"

"Nobody. I go of my own accord."

"Well, I never have seen the like of you before," said the man, still laughing good-naturedly. "Where, then, is your home, my boy?"

"I do not know exactly. It may be on the Lake of Garda," was the serious answer.

"What sort of reply is that?"

So saying, the coachman looked with some curiosity at the little figure before him, which certainly did not betray any signs of being neglected. On the contrary, the head, with its black curly hair, and the nice Sunday suit of clothes, gave the lad a very genteel appearance; and his delicate features and earnest eyes bore unmistakable evidence to something noble in his character, and any one who looked at him once was certain to repeat the glance with pleasure.

Such was also the case with the driver. He gazed steadfastly at Rico, and presently said, kindly, "You carry your passport in your face, my boy; and it is not a bad one either, even if you do not know where you belong. What will you give me now, if I will carry you along with me down yonder, on the box?"

Rico stared, for he could scarcely believe his ears at these words. To sit on that high post-wagon, and drive down into the valley! Such luck could never, never be his; of that he was sure. Besides, what had he to give the coachman in exchange?

"I have only my fiddle in the world, and I cannot give that away," he said sadly, after thinking a while.

"Well, I should not know what to do with that box," laughed the driver "Come along. We will get up there, and you may play me a little music."

Rico could not trust his ears; but, sure enough, the coachman pushed him up over the wheel to the top of the coach, climbing up after him. The passengers had all taken their places, the doors were closed, and away they rolled down the road.--the well-known road over which Rico had so often longingly gazed, wishing that he could travel it.

Now his wish was realized. High up between heaven and earth he seemed to be flying, and could not believe that he was not in a dream.

The coachman was revolving in his own mind the question of the boy's belongings.

"Just tell me, now, you little travelling bundle, where your father lives."

He asked this after having cracked his whip many times in succession as loud as he could.

"He is dead."

"Oh, dear! Well, where is your mother, then?"

"She is dead, too."

"Well, there is always a grandfather and a grandmother, or something. Where are yours?"

"All dead."

"At any rate, everybody has some brothers or sisters; where are yours, I should like to know?"

"All are dead," was the sorrowfully repeated answer.

When the driver had convinced himself that they were all gone, he ceased his questions about the relatives, and began in another direction with, "What was your father's name?"

"Henrico Trevillo of Peschiera, on the Lake of Garda."

At last the driver thought he had got at the root of the matter, and said to himself this boy had strayed away, or been carried away, from his home down below there, and it is a good thing for him to get carried back where he belongs; and he thought no more about the affair.

Presently they passed the first very steep bit of the hill, and came to an even stretch of ground, and the driver said, "Now, musician, let us have a jolly song to cheer the way."

Full of satisfaction, and much elated at his high position on his throne under the blue heaven, the boy took his instrument and began to sing in his strong, clear tones,--

"Little lambkins, come down."

Now it happened that there were three students seated up on the top of the post-wagon: they were off on a vacation trip, and very merry.

So when Rico carolled forth Stineli's song in his gayest manner, they all burst out laughing and shouted, "Stop, singer, stop, and begin over again; we want to sing with you."

Rico obeyed, and the jolly students joined in with all their might,--

"And the lambkins, and the lambkins,"--

and laughed so extravagantly all the time that they drowned the sound of Rico's fiddle completely. And then one of them would take up the words and sing alone,--

"And if they forgot it,   It hurt not a bit."

And then the others joined in, and sang as loudly as possible,--

"And the lambkins, and the lambkins."

And so they went on for a long time. If Rico paused a little, they shouted, "Go on, fiddler; don't stop yet," and threw little pieces of money to him over and over again, until he had quite a heap in his cap.

Within the coach the passengers opened the windows, and stuck their heads out to listen to the merry singing.

Rico started off afresh, and the students also. They divided the song into solos and chorus; and the solo sang very solemnly,--

"And one lake, like another, From water is made."

And then again,--

"And because they forgot it, It hurt not a bit."

And the chorus took it up with,--

"And the lambkins, and the lambkins."

Then they laughed so that they were almost dead, and were forced to be still for very fatigue and want of breath.

Presently the driver stopped, for it was time for the horses to rest, and also dinner-time. While the good man helped Rico down, he held the little fellow's cap firmly for him, for it had a lot of money in it, and the boy was busy enough with holding his fiddle carefully.

The coachman was perfectly delighted when he saw the money, and said, as he gave Rico the cap, "That is first rate; now you can have a good dinner."

The students leaped down one after the other, and crowded around the fiddler to have a look at him, for they could not see him very well on the top of the coach; and when they discovered what a tiny manikin he was, they began to make merry again. Judging from his voice, they had expected to see a large, strong musician; and the sight of this child seemed to make the fun twice as funny.

They took the little fellow up between them, and carried him with singing and laughter into the inn. There they seated him at the table between two gentlemen, and said that he was their guest; and they all helped him one after the other, and put huge pieces upon his plate, for no one would be outdone by the others in serving him; and the boy had certainly never eaten such a dinner in all his life as he ate that day.

"Tell us where you learned your beautiful song?" asked one of three.

"Stineli made it up," replied Rico, very seriously.

The students looked at each other at these words, and burst out again with laughter.

"So Stineli made it up, did she? Then we must drink her health over it."

Rico had to join in drinking the toast, and was nothing loath to drink to Stineli's health.

But now the time for resting and eating was over; and while they were all taking their places to go on their journey, a stout man came towards Rico,--a man who had such a big stick in his hand, that it looked as if he had torn up a young tree for his walking-stick. He was dressed in a thick, golden-brown stuff from head to foot.

"Come here, little one," he said to Rico. "How nicely you did sing! I heard you here, inside the coach; and my business is also with sheep, for, you know, I am a sheep-dealer; and I want to give you something, because you can sing about them so prettily."

With these words he put a big piece of silver in Rico's hand, for the cap had been emptied by this time, and the contents transferred to the boy's pocket.

After this the man got into the coach, and the driver lifted Rico up to his high seat as if the boy had been a mere feather, and off they went.

As soon as the speed of the start had a little abated, the students called for more music, and Rico played every thing that he could remember ever having heard his father play; and at the end he played,--

"I sing to thee with heart and voice."

But this tune must have put the students to sleep, for every thing became quite still; and at last the riddle was silent. The evening breeze stirred gently, and the stars climbed silently up into the sky one after the other, until they were shining brightly in every direction.

Rico looked about, and thought of Stineli, of the grandmother, of what they were now doing; and it occurred to him that this was the very time at which the prayer-bell usually rang, and when they were saying "Our Father." He did the same, to be with them in that, at least: folded his hands, and said his prayer piously under the brilliant heavens.

CHAPTER XII.
IT STILL GOES ON.

At last Rico also fell asleep. He only awoke when the driver took hold of him to lift him down. All the passengers descended; and the three students came to the lad, shook him kindly by the hand, and wished a happy journey. One of them called out, "Greet Stineli very kindly for us." Then they disappeared up one of the streets, and Rico could hear them as they sang merrily,--

"And the lambkins, and the lambkins,"

Rico now stood alone in the darkness. He had not the slightest idea where he was, nor of what he ought to do next. He presently remembered that he had not even thanked the kind coachman who had allowed him to come all this way on the coach, and he felt that he must do that at once.

The coachman and his horses were both invisible, and nothing but darkness was about the boy. At last he espied a lantern hanging up somewhere in the distance, and went towards the light. It was hanging on the stable-door, and the horses were just then brought in. Near the door stood the man with the thick stick. He seemed to be waiting for the driver; so Rico took his stand near by, and waited too.

Probably the sheep-dealer did not recognize the little fiddler in the darkness; but suddenly he exclaimed, quite surprised, "What! is that you, little one? Where are you going to pass the night?"

"I do not know where," replied the boy.

"Well, I never heard of such a thing; at eleven o'clock at night, and a little scrap of a boy like you in a strange place"--

The sheep-dealer seemed to speak in a great hurry, for he could scarcely breathe in his excitement; neither did he finish his sentence, for the driver entered the stable at that moment, and Rico went up to him at once, saying, "I want to thank you for bringing me along with you."

"You have come just in the nick of time. I had almost forgotten you while I was looking after my horses, and I wanted to hand you over to an acquaintance. I was thinking of asking you, good friend," he continued, turning towards the dealer, "if you would not take this little chap along with you, as you are going to Bergamo. He wants to go somewhere on the Lake of Garda. He is one of those who belong here or there. You understand, don't you?"

The sheep-dealer thought of the stories he had heard of lost or stolen children. He looked with pity at Rico, standing in the dim light of the lantern, and said, "He does look as if he were not in exactly the clothes that belong to him. He would become a richer dress, I am sure. I will take him with me."

When he had talked over the sheep-trade a little with the coachman they parted, and the dealer made a sign to Rico that he should follow him.

After a short walk, the man entered an inn, where he seated himself in a corner of the eating-room with the boy beside him.

"Now let us look at your possessions," he said to Rico, "so that we can see what they will allow you to have. Where are you going on the lake?"

"To Peschiera, on the Lake of Garda."

This was Rico's never-failing answer. He drew out his money from his pocket,--a nice little pile of small coins it was, and the big silver bit on the top of all.

"Have you only that one bit of silver?" asked the dealer.

"Yes; only that one. You gave me that," replied the boy.

It pleased the man to think that he was the only one who had given silver; and he was also pleased that the lad was aware of the fact. He felt as if he wanted to give him something more. Just at this moment his supper was placed before him, and the kindly man nodded to his little companion, saying, "I will pay for this, and for your night's lodging also; so you need not touch your little fortune until to-morrow."

Rico was so tired out with all the fiddling and singing, and the long journey, that he could scarcely eat; and as soon as he reached the big bedroom where he was to pass the night with his protector, he was asleep the moment he had put his head on the pillow.

Early the following morning, Rico was awakened from a sound sleep by a powerful grasp. He sprang quickly out of bed. His companion stood ready dressed for the journey, with his big stick in his hand.

It was not long, however, before Rico was also ready, with his fiddle tucked under his arm. They went into the dining-room, and the dealer called for coffee at once. He recommended the lad to make a good meal then; for they had a long journey before them, he said, and one that created an appetite.

When they had breakfasted to their satisfaction, they sallied forth; and, after a little, came round a sharp corner; and how Rico did open his big eyes! for there, before him, lay a great shining lake; and much excited, he shouted out, "Now we are on the Lake of Garda!"

"Not for a long time yet, my boy. This is the Lake of Como."

They went on board a boat, and sailed for several hours after this; and Rico looked about him,--at the sun-bathed shores, and then at the blue waters; and he felt at home at last.

Presently he took his piece of silver from his pocket, and put it down on the table before the dealer.

"What does this mean? Have you too much money by you?" asked the man, who was looking on in surprise, his arms supported on his big stick.

"I must pay to-day," said Rico. "You said so yesterday."

"You are very attentive to what is said to you. That is a very good thing; but that is not the way to do, to put your money down on a table like that. Give it to me."

He took it, and went over to pay for their passage; but when he drew out his heavy leathern purse, full of silver pieces,--for he was doing a large business in selling sheep,--he could not find the heart to take the poor lad's solitary bit of silver; and he brought it back again with the ticket, saying, "There, you can find better use for your money to-morrow. Now you are with me, but who knows how it will be after this? When you are alone down there, and I am not with you any more, shall you be able to find the house where you are going?"

"No; I do not know any thing about the house," replied Rico.

The man was secretly much surprised, and the lad's story seemed very mysterious to him. He did not let this appear, however, and asked no further questions. He said to himself that he should not probably find out any thing more at present, but would ask the coachman about it the next time they met. He probably knew the truth, even better than the child himself did. He felt very sorry for the little fellow, who would soon be deprived of his protection too.

When the boat stopped, the man took Rico's hand in his, saying, "Now I shall not lose you, and you can keep up with me better, for we must hurry along; they won't wait for us."

It was as much as the little fellow could do to keep up with his friend. He did not turn to look to the right hand nor the left, but presently stopped before some strange-looking wagons on wheels. They mounted the step, Rico behind his companion; and the former entered a railroad carriage for the first time.

They flew along for several hours, until at last the dealer stood up, and said, "Now I must go. We are in Bergamo, and you are to stay here quietly; for I have arranged it all for you. You have only to get out when you get there."

"Then shall I be at Peschiera, on the Lake of Garda?" asked Rice.

His companion replied in the affirmative. At last Rico understood--what he had not clearly seen before--how much kindness the dealer had shown to him, and the boy felt very sorry that they must part.

After this Rico sat alone in his corner, and had plenty of time for day-dreaming; for nobody troubled him in any way, although the train had stopped at several stations since his companion left him.

At last the conductor came in, took Rico by the arm, and led him quickly to the door, and lifted him down the steps; then, pointing towards the heights in the distance, he said briefly, "Peschiera;" and in a twinkling he was back again in the carriage, and disappeared in the train as it steamed off.

CHAPTER XIII.
ON THE DISTANT, BEAUTIFUL LAKE.

Rico went forward a little way from the building at which the train had stopped, and looked about. This white house, the barren square in front of it, the straight road in the distance, were all new and strange to his eyes. He had not seen any of them before; and he said to himself, "I have not come to the right place after all." He went sadly down the road between the trees, however, until presently the road made a turn, and the boy stood as if transfixed, and believed himself dreaming, for before him lay the lake, heavenly blue in the brilliant sunlight, with its warm, still shores; and yonder were the mountains, and the sunny bay was there, where the friendly houses sparkled in the distance.

Now he knew where he was. He had seen all this before, he had stood in this very place, he knew the trees perfectly well; but where was the cottage? It must have stood there, close to where he now was, but it was not visible.

The old road was there below. Oh! he knew that well; and there, there were the great shining red flowers with such green leaves. A little stone bridge ought to be there, somewhere over the outlet of the lake: he had often passed over that little bridge, but could not see it where he stood, however.

Rico started off, as if driven by the longing that now took possession of him. Down the road he ran; and over there,--yes, that was the little stone bridge. Every thing came back to him: there he had crossed, and somebody held him by the hand,--his mother. Suddenly his mother's face came before his eyes quite distinctly;

he had never seen it so clearly before. He remembered how she had stood there and looked at him with loving eyes. It all came back to his mind with a rush.

He threw himself down on the ground by the bridge, and cried and sobbed aloud, "O mother! where are you, mother? Where is my home, mother?"

He lay there for a long, long time, and cried until his great sorrow was somewhat stilled. He thought his heart must burst, and as if all the grief that had been hitherto pent up within his bosom must now find an outlet.

When at last he raised himself from the ground, the sun had already declined in the heavens, and the golden twilight lay over the lake. The mountains were turning purple, and a sunny mist lay all over the shores. This was the way his lake had always looked to Rico in his dreams, only the reality was even more lovely than he had remembered it.

And his great wish rose again in his mind as he sat there, "Oh, if I could show this to Stineli!"

At last the sun sunk below the horizon, and the light slowly died out. Rico arose, and passed along the road towards the red flowers. A narrow lane branched off from the main road at this place. There they stood, one bush after another: it looked like a great garden. There was, truly, only an open fence about the whole; and within the flowers, the trees, and the grape-vines were all growing together.

At the farther end stood a pretty house with wide open doors; and in the garden a lad was moving about cutting big bunches of golden grapes now from this vine, now from that, all the while whistling merrily.

Rico gazed at the flowers, and thought, "If Stineli could only see them!" He stood for a long time thoughtfully by the fence. Presently the lad espied him, and called out, "Come in, fiddler; and play a pretty song, if you know one."

The lad spoke in Italian, and it produced a strange sensation in Rico's mind: he understood what he heard, but he never could have said it himself. He entered the garden, and the lad began to try to talk with him; but when he found that Rico could not reply, he pointed towards the open door, giving Rico to understand that he was to go there to play.

When Rico approached the door, he found that it opened directly into a bedroom. A little bed stood within, near which was seated a woman who was knitting with red yarn. Rico placed himself before the threshold, and began to play and sing his song,--

"Little lambkins, come down."

When he had finished, the pale face of a little boy was suddenly raised from the pillows of the bed; and Rico heard the words,--

"Play again."

Rico played another tune.

"Play again" was repeated. This went on for five or six times, until Rico had exhausted his stock of songs and tunes; and he put his fiddle under his arm, and was moving away, when the little boy began to call out piteously,--

"Oh, do stay! Do play again! Play something else!" Then the woman stood up, and came towards Rico.

She placed something in his hand, and at first he did not understand what she wanted; but presently he remembered what Stineli had said, that if he went to a door, and played on his fiddle, the people would give him something. The woman asked him kindly where he came from, and where he was going to; but he could not answer her. She then asked if he were with his parents? He shook his head. If he were alone? He nodded assent. Where he was going so late in the evening? Rico shook his head, to denote uncertainty. A great pity took possession of the woman for the little stranger; and she called to the boy who worked in the garden, and bade him conduct the fiddler to the inn of the "Golden Sun." Perhaps the landlord would understand his language, for he had been away in foreign parts for a long time. She bade the gardener to say to the landlord that she wished him to let the lad stay there over night, that she would pay for it; and, in the morning, set the little fellow off in the right direction towards his destination. He was so young,--"only a little older than my boy," she added, compassionately; and also would the landlord give the boy something to eat.

Again the child on the bed called out, "He must play again;" and would not stop until his mother said, "He will come again. Now he must sleep, and you too."

The gardener walked on in advance of Rico, who knew, however, what was to be done; for he had understood what the woman said perfectly.

In about ten minutes they had reached the town. In one of the little streets the gardener entered a house, and proceeded at once to the dining-room, which was filled with tobacco-smoke, and with men seated at little tables all about.

Then the gardener gave his message, to which the landlord replied, "It is all right." The landlady came too, and both looked Rico over from head to foot. When the guests at the neighboring tables espied the fiddle under Rico's arm, several of them called out together, "There is music!" And another one shouted, "Play something, boy, quickly; something gay!" And they all began to shout for music so noisily that the landlord could hardly make Rico hear him when he asked what language he spoke, and whence he came. Rico replied in his own language that he came down over the Maloja, that he could understand every thing that was said to him, but could not reply in the same language. The landlord understood him, and said that he had been up there in the mountains, and they would have a little conversation later; but now the boy must really play something, for the guests called for music incessantly.

Rico, obedient as ever, began to play, and also to sing his own song as usual. But the company did not understand the words, and the tune seemed very dull to them also. Some began to make jokes and noises, while others called for something different,--a dance, or a pretty tune.

Rico sang every verse of his song to the very end; for when he had once begun it, he would not stop until it was finished properly. When he had finished, he bethought himself. He knew no dance music, so that was out of the question. The hymn he had learned from the grandmother was very slow, and they would not understand that either. Then he remembered, and began the air,--

"Una Sera
  In Peschiera."

Scarcely had he brought forth the first notes of this tune, when every thing became still; and in a moment or two voices broke forth from the different tables round about the room, and they sang in chorus as the boy had never yet heard any one sing. He became excited presently, and played with great feeling, while the men sang enthusiastically; and as soon as one verse was ended, Rico began the music for the next without hesitating, for he had learned, from hearing his father play it, exactly how the accompaniment should be, and when to stop. When he had reached the finale, such a storm of applause broke forth that the boy was quite overwhelmed. All the men called out and shouted, striking their fists upon the tables for pleasure; and then they all came about little Rico with their glasses, and they all wanted to drink with him. Some took him by the shoulders, and all shouted at him, and made such a racket with their surprise and pleasure, that Rico became very much frightened, and turned paler and paler every moment.

What had he done, however, but play their own Peschiera song, that belonged to them alone, and which no stranger could ever learn; and this child had played it as firmly and correctly as if he had been a Peschierana. Such a wonderful event was enough to arouse these lively fellows to the utmost; and they could not cease talking about it, and wondering about this strange little fiddler, and drinking with him, to express their friendliness.

At last the landlady interposed. She brought a plate full of rice, and a big piece of chicken. She beckoned Rico aside, saying to the men they must let him have a little quiet now; he needed food; he was as pale as chalk from excitement. She placed the dish upon a little table in one corner, and encouraged him to eat heartily: she was sure he needed it, he was such a little scrap. To tell the truth, Rico did enjoy his supper wonderfully well. Since the coffee in the morning, not a mouthful had passed his lips; and so much had happened to excite him too.

As soon as he had eaten all that there was upon his plate, his poor little eyes closed from fatigue, and he had the greatest difficulty in keeping them open long enough to answer the landlord's questions of where he belonged, and where he was going, while he also praised the child's music. Rico answered that he belonged to nobody, and was going nowhere.

The landlord spoke kindly and encouragingly to the boy, telling him that he should be cared for that night, and in the morning he could go to see Mrs. Menotti, who had sent him there. She was a good, kind woman, said the landlord, who could perhaps employ him in her household, if he had no place to go to where he belonged.

His wife, who stood by, plucked him constantly by the sleeve, trying to stop him from talking; but he finished what he had to say, nevertheless, for he had no idea what she meant by it all.

Pretty soon the men at the tables began to clamor again: they were calling for their song.

The landlady, however, asserted herself. "No, no! on Sunday you shall have it again; the child is tired to death." So saying, she took Rico by the hand, and led him up into a big room where the harnesses hung. A big heap of corn lay in one corner, and a bed stood in the other. In a very few moments the boy was fast asleep.

Later, when every thing had become quite silent in the house, the landlord sat at the little table where Rico had eaten his supper, and before him stood his wife, for she was still busy in clearing away the tables; and she said with great earnestness, "You must not send him back again to Mrs. Menotti. Such a boy as that will be most useful to me in every possible way; and did not you notice how beautifully he fiddled? They were all crazy about it. Look out! he is a far better player than any of our three; and he will learn to play for dancing in no time; and you will have a musician to whom you need pay nothing, and who will play every evening when they dance; and you can let him out also to go to the other places. Don't you let him slip through your fingers. He is a pretty little fellow, and I like him. We must keep him ourselves."

"Well, I am satisfied," said the landlord, and understood that his wife had made a hit this time that was sure to turn out well.

CHAPTER XIV.
NEW FRIENDSHIPS FORMED, WHILE THE OLD ONES ARE NOT FORGOTTEN.

The next morning, the landlady of the "Golden Sun" stood on the doorstep of her inn, and looked at the heavens to read the signs of the probable weather, and to think over the experiences of the night before. Presently the gardener's boy from Mrs. Menotti's came along. He was both master and servant over the lovely, fruitful property of Mrs. Menotti; for he understood both the care of the garden and the cultivation of the farm, and he looked after and directed all the work himself, and had an easy and good place with her. He was contented, and whistled incessantly.

However, while he stood before the landlady, he stopped for a little, and said, if the little musician of the evening before had not gone away, he was to go over to

Mrs. Menotti again, because her little boy wanted to hear him fiddle some more.

"Yes, yes; if Mrs. Menotti is not in a great hurry,"--while she put her arms on her hips, to show that she, at any rate, was not pressed for time. "At the present moment the little musician is sleeping upstairs in his good bed; and I, for one, do not wish to have him disturbed. You may say to Mrs. Menotti that I will send him to her presently. He is not going away. I have taken him under my charge for good and all; for he is a deserted orphan, and does not know where to go; and now he will be well cared for," added she, with emphasis.

The gardener went off with this message.

Rico was allowed to sleep as long as he wanted to; for the landlady was a good-natured woman, though, to be sure, she thought first of her own profit, and after-wards was willing to help others to theirs. When the boy awoke, at last, from his long sleep, his fatigue had quite disappeared; and he came running down the stairs as fresh as possible. The landlady made a sign for him to come into the kitchen, and placed a big bowl of coffee before him, with a nice yellow corn-cake, saying,--

"You can have this every morning, if you will, and something much better at dinner and supper time; for then there is cooking for the guests, and there is always something left over. You can do errands for me in return for it; and you can make this your home, and have your bedroom to yourself, and not be obliged to go wan-dering about in the world. Now it lies with you to decide."

To this Rico replied, simply,--

"Yes, I will;" for he could say that in the language in which the landlady spoke.

Now she conducted him through the whole house, through the out-buildings, the stable, into the vegetable-garden and the hen-house; and she explained the situ-ation of all the places to him, and told him where he must turn to go to the grocer and to the shoemaker, and to all the important trades-people in fact. Rico listened attentively; and, to test his understanding, the landlady sent him at once to three or four places, to fetch a variety of things, such as oil, soap, thread, and a boot that had been mended; for she noticed that the boy could say single words perfectly well.

All these errands were done to her perfect satisfaction; and at last she said, "Now you may go over to Mrs. Menotti with your fiddle, and stay there until the evening."

Rico was delighted at this permission; for he would pass by the lake, and see the beautiful flowers he loved so well.

As soon as he reached the lake-side, over he ran to the little bridge, and seated himself there to watch the beautiful water, and the mountains bathed in golden mist; and he could scarcely tear himself away from it all.

But he did; for he realized now that he had duties toward the landlady, and must obey her, because she gave him food and lodging.

As he entered the garden, the little boy heard his footstep, for the door was always open; and he called out,--

"Come here, and play some more."

Mrs. Menotti came out, and gave her hand kindly to Rico, and drew him into the room with her. It was a large room, and you could look through the wide door-way out into the garden where the flowers were to be seen. The little bed on which the sick child lay was directly opposite the door; and there were only chests and tables and chairs in the room, but no other beds. At night the child was carried into the neighboring room, and his bed also, and was placed there beside his mother for the night; and in the morning he was carried back again, bed and all. For in this large room the sun shone brightly, making long shining stripes across the floor that made a dancing pattern on the ground, and amused the child amazingly. Near the bed stood two little crutches; and now and then his mother lifted the little cripple from his bed, placed the crutches under his arms, and led him about the room once or twice; for he could not walk, nor even stand alone. His little legs were quite para-lyzed, and he had never been able to use them at all.

When Rico entered the room, the child pulled himself into a sitting position by means of a long rope that hung down over his bed from the ceiling for that purpose; for he could not sit up without assistance.

Rico went to the bedside, and looked at the child in silence. Such little thin arms and small slender fingers, and such a pale little face, Rico had never seen; and two big eyes looked forth from the face, and gazed at Rico as if they would pierce him through and through; for the child, who seldom saw any thing new, and longed for variety with all his heart, examined every thing that came in his way very sharply.

"What is your name?" asked the child.

"Rico."

"Mine is Silvio. How old are you?"

"Almost eleven."

"And so am I," said the child.

"O Silvio! what are you saying?" said his mother at this. "You are not quite four yet. Time does not go so fast as that."

"Play something more."

The mother seated herself by the bedside. Rico placed himself at a little distance, and began to play on his fiddle. Silvio could not have enough of it; and no sooner had Rico finished one piece than he shouted, "Play another." Six times each, at the very least, had all the pieces been repeated, when Mrs. Menotti went out, and returned with a plate filled with yellow grapes, saying that Rico ought to rest, and sit down by the bedside, and eat some grapes with Silvio.

She went out into the garden herself while the children were eating, and was glad to be able to do so, and to attend to various little matters of her own; for it was seldom that she could leave the bedside of her little cripple, for he would not let her leave him, and cried bitterly for her to return; so it was a real blessing to her to be able to get away for a few moments.

The two boys soon came to a most excellent understanding of each other; for Rico could reply very well to Silvio's questions, and managed to make himself very well understood, even when he could not find exactly the proper words, and it was very amusing to Silvio to talk with him. His mother had plenty of time to look at all the flower-beds, and to examine the fine fig-trees in the orchard, and to overlook every thing, without being called for once by her little boy.

When she returned to the house, however, and Rico arose to take his departure, Silvio set up a great shout, and clung to Rico with both hands, and would not let him go until he had promised to come back the next day, and every day. But Mrs. Menotti was a cautious woman. She had understood the message sent by the landlady as it was intended, and quieted her son, promising him to go herself to the landlady to talk with her; because Rico, she said, was not able to promise to do any thing himself, but must obey the landlady in every thing. At last the child released Rico, and gave him his hand; and the latter reluctantly left the room. He would have vastly preferred to remain there where it was quiet and neat, and where Silvio and his mother were so kind to him.

Several days had slipped by, when, towards evening, Mrs. Menotti made her appearance, dressed in her best attire, in the doorway of the "Golden Sun;" and the landlady ran joyfully to meet her, and led her up into the upper hall. When they were there, Mrs. Menotti asked very politely if it would inconvenience the landlady very much to allow Rico to come over to her two or three times in the week towards evening, he was so amusing, and entertained her little sick son so well. She would gladly recompense the landlady in any way she might think desirable.

It flattered the landlady to have the handsomely dressed Mrs. Menotti thus asking a favor of her; and it was quickly arranged that Rico should go to Mrs. Menotti on every free evening that he had; and in return, Mrs. Menotti promised to provide the orphan's clothing, which pleased the landlady extremely; for now she had really nothing to pay out for the little boy, and he brought her in a great deal of money. So it was arranged to the entire satisfaction of the two women, and they took leave of each other in very friendly terms.

In this way passed many days. Rico could soon speak Italian as if he had always spoken it. And, in truth, he had once spoken it as his native language, so one thing after another came back to him; and as he had a good ear, he soon spoke exactly like an Italian born, so that all who knew him to be a stranger wondered at him. He was very useful to the landlady,--more so even than she had expected would be the case,--for he was so neat and orderly: quite as much so as she herself, if not more, for she was not very patient over her work; and when preparations were necessary for a *fete* or for a wedding, Rico was called upon to do it, for he had a great deal of taste, and knew how to carry it out in decorations. If he had any errand to do abroad he was back again in an incredibly short time, for he never stopped to chatter by the way. If people questioned him, he always turned on his heel and left them. This pleased the landlady mightily when she noticed it, and it created such a feeling of respect for the lad in her mind, that she herself did not question him; and so it came to pass that, indeed, nobody really knew how he came to Peschiera. But a story was spread abroad, that everybody believed, to the effect that he had been left an orphan without protection in the mountains, and neglected and mishandled, so that at last he ran away, suffering many things on the long journey until he reached Peschiera, where the inhabitants were not rough as they are in the mountains, and that he was glad to remain there with them. Whenever the landlady told his story, she did not fail to add, "He deserves it, too,--all the kindness that we show him, and his comfortable home under our roof."

Now the first "dance Sunday" of the season had come, and such an enormous crowd of guests assembled in the "Golden Sun," that there seemed a great doubt if they could all be accommodated there; but everybody wished to see and to hear the little stranger who played so wonderfully; and also they who had heard him on the evening of his arrival were the very first to come, and were impatient for him to play their song again.

The landlady ran hither and thither in her excitement, and glowed and glistened in her heat, as if she were herself the "Golden Sun;" and when she met her husband, she always said triumphantly, "Did not I tell you so?"

Rico heard "dance music" for the first time played by the three fiddlers who came to the inn; but he caught the melodies at once, and had no trouble in playing them, and never forgot them. for they were so often repeated during the long "dance evening," that they became very familiar to him.

After the dancing they wanted their Peschiera song, with Rico's accompaniment; and even if there seemed to be a deal of noise all the early part of the evening, now, in truth, it had really just begun; and they became so excited that little quiet Rico was frightened, and thought they would end by killing each other certainly.

But it was all in friendly wise. He came in for his share, and was so stormily applauded, and his musical performance was hailed with such ear-splitting cries of approval, that his only thought at last was, "Oh, when will this have an end!" for nothing was so very unpleasant to the boy as boisterousness.

In the evening the landlady said to her husband, "Did you notice Rico could play all the pieces with the musicians? Next time we shall only need two fiddlers." And the man replied, well pleased, "We must give Rico something."

Two days later there was a dance in Desenzano, and Rico was sent over there with the fiddlers. Now he was let out for hire. The same noise and merriment was repeated; and, although they did not call for the Peschiera song in Desenzano, still there were plenty of other songs just as noisy, and Rico thought only from beginning to end, "If it were but over!"

He brought a whole pocketful of money home with him, which he poured out in a heap on the table without even counting it, for he thought it was all the landlady's by right; and she praised him in return, and placed a big piece of apple-pie before him for supper. On Sunday again there was dancing in Riva; but this was a pleasure to Rico, for Riva was the spot over across the lake which could be seen from Peschiera, looking like a peaceful little bay, and where the pretty white houses looked so friendly and attractive.

The musicians were rowed all together across the lake in an open boat under the clear heavens; and Rico thought, "Oh, if I could be rowed across here, with Stineli by my side! How astonished she would be at the lake, whose beauty she would not believe in."

But once on the other shore, the noise began again, and the boy became impatient to be off; for the view of Riva from across the lake, lying in the lovely light of evening, was far more beautiful than being there in the midst of the noise and tumult.

However, when there were no dances at which he must play, the lad was always allowed to go in the evening to little Silvio, and to remain as long as he wished; for the landlady was anxious to show her willingness to accommodate Mrs. Menotti. This was always a pleasure to Rico. Whenever he passed along the lake-side, he went over to the little stone bridge, and sat there for a while on the ground; for this was the only place in the world where he had a home-like feeling, because what he saw there he had seen before, and also here the vision of his mother rose most clearly before his memory.

There she had certainly stood by the water-side, and washed something, while she would look around at him occasionally, and say a few loving words; and he was always sitting, he remembered, in that very place where he now sat. He was always most unwilling to leave this spot, but the knowledge that Silvio was constantly listening for him drove him onward.

When he entered the garden, he had also a feeling of contentment; and entered the neat, quiet house with pleasure. Mrs. Menotti had a more truly friendly manner toward him than anybody else, and he was fully sensible of her kindness. She felt the warmest pity for the lonely orphan, as she called him; for she had also heard the story of his escape as it was current in the neighborhood. She never asked him questions concerning his life in the mountains, however; for she thought it would arouse sad memories in his mind. She felt, also, that Rico did not receive the care that a lad of his age and quiet disposition really needed; but she was sensible that she could do nothing in that direction, only to have him with her as often and as long as possible. Often she would place her hand on his head, saying sadly, "Poor little orphan!"

To Silvio, Rico grew more and more necessary every day. Early in the morning he began to fret for him; and when his pain came on he became very restless, and could not be pacified until Rico came. For, since Rico had mastered the language thoroughly, he had developed an inexhaustible fund of stories that delighted the little invalid beyond measure.

Stineli was the theme on which Rico most often fell, and it made him so happy even to talk about her, that he became animated and quite transfigured in the recital. He knew hundreds of stories, such as when Stineli caught little Sami by the leg, once on a time, just as he was about to fall into the water-butt, and how she held him with all her might, while they both screamed as loud as they could until their father came slowly to their aid,--for he always moved slowly. He said that children did nothing but scream: it was their nature, and did not mean that they were in trouble. And he told Silvio how Stineli could cut out figures from paper for Peterli, make all sorts of furniture and things for the baby-house for Urschli from moss, and bits of wood, or any thing that came to hand.

And how they all called and clamored for their elder sister when they were ill, because she told them such wonderful stories that they quite forgot their pains while listening. Rico also told the story of his beautiful walks with Stineli, and became so much excited in his talk that Silvio caught the inspiration, and asked for more and more, calling out, "Tell me about Stineli again!" as soon as Rico paused to take breath. One evening the child broke out into the wildest excitement when Rico took his leave, saying that he would not be able to come on the following day nor on Sunday. Silvio shrieked for his mother as if the house were burning, and he were in the midst of the flames; and as she came hurrying to him from the garden, almost frightened to death at his noise, he declared "Rico should *not* go again back to the inn; but must stay always, always with them. You must stay here, Rico. You must never, never go away!"

But Rico said, "I would stay most gladly; but I cannot."

Mrs. Menotti was much perplexed. She knew very well how valuable Rico's services were to the inn-keepers, and that she could never obtain him under any consideration. She tried to silence her little son to the best of her ability, while she drew Rico to her side, saying, as was her wont, "Poor little orphan!" Whereupon Silvio called out angrily, "What is an orphan? I want to be an orphan too."

These words aroused his mother; and she cried out, in her turn, "Silvio, you wicked child! Do you know that an orphan is a wretched child, who has neither father nor mother, and no home on all the earth?"

Rico's black eyes were fixed on Mrs. Menotti's face, and then seemed to grow blacker and more black every minute; but she did not notice them. She had ceased to think about the lad while she was giving this explanation of an orphan to her son. The little fellow slipped quietly and unperceived away.

When Mrs. Menotti observed his absence, she thought he had stolen away in order not to excite Silvio further by taking leave, and she was pleased at his thoughtfulness. Seating herself by the bedside of her child, she said, "I want to make you understand how it is, Silvio; and then you will stop being so naughty, I hope. It is not possible to take a child away from any one; and, even if I took Rico from the landlady, she would have a right to come and take you away from me. Then you would not be able to see the garden nor the flowers any more, and would have to sleep quite alone in the room with the harnesses where Rico dislikes so much to sleep. Don't you remember what he has told you about that? What would you do then?"

"Come right home again," said the child decidedly; but he was quite still after that, and soon lay down and slept.

Rico passed through the garden, along the street, and down to the lake. There he sat down on his favorite spot, leaned his head upon his hands, and said, in tones of utter despair, "Now I know the truth, mother. Now I know that I have no home,--none in the whole world."

And there he sat until late in the night, alone with his sad thoughts; and would have rather remained there forever, but he was obliged to go back into his uncomfortable bedroom at last.

CHAPTER XV.
SILVIO'S WISHES PRODUCE RESULTS.

But the excitement had not subsided in Silvio's mind, by any means; and now that he knew that two days must elapse before Rico could come again, he began to cry early in the morning, "Rico won't come to-day! Rico won't come to-day!" and scarcely ceased until the evening, and the second day it was the same, but on the third,--he was tired out by that time, and seemed like a little heap of straw, that the least spark could have reduced to ashes.

In the evening Rico made his appearance, quite worn out with the noise and tumult of the dances for which he had been obliged to play. Since he had fully real- ized that he had no home on the earth, the thought of Stineli had become of more importance than ever, and he said to himself,--

"There is only Stineli in the whole world to whom I belong, or who troubles her head about me!" And he felt a terrible homesickness for Stineli. He had scarcely reached the side of Silvio's bed when he said, "Do you know, Silvio, with Stineli only can one feel perfectly well, and nowhere else." These words were scarcely out of his mouth before the little invalid hoisted himself up like a flash, calling out at the top of his lungs, "Mother, I must have Stineli; Stineli must come; only with Stineli can one feel perfectly well, and nowhere else."

His mother came at his call; and as she had often listened to Rico's stories about Stineli and her brothers and sisters with great interest, she knew at once what they were talking about, and replied, "Yes, yes; it would suit me very well. I could find great use for Stineli for you, and for myself, if I only had her here."

But such an indefinite way of talking did not suit Silvio in the least, for he was interested, heart and soul, in the matter.

"You can have her at once," he cried out. "Rico knows where she is: he must go to fetch her. I want her every day, and always. To-morrow Rico must go to get her: he knows where."

Now that his mother saw that the little fellow had thought the whole thing out, and was really in serious earnest about it, she tried to turn his attention away, and to introduce other thoughts into his mind, for she had often heard the story of the incredible adventures Rico passed through on his journey over the mountains, and of the wonder of his having survived and come down safely, and that the mountaineer were a fearful and wild people. She was, therefore, fully persuaded that nobody could bring a girl away, and certainly not a tender little lad like Rico. He might meet a sad fate, and be lost altogether, if he attempted any thing of the kind; and then she would be responsible for it all. She would not run that risk,--she thought she had enough to bear already.

So she placed all the impossibility of the affair before Silvio's eyes, and told him of the terrible circumstances, and of the wicked men whom Rico would have to encounter, and who might ruin him. But nothing had the slightest effect. The little fellow had set his heart upon this thing as he never had upon any thing before; and whatever his mother brought forward, and no matter how anxiously she insisted, the moment she ceased the child said, "Rico must go to fetch her: he knows where to find her."

Then his mother replied, "And even if he does know, do you mean to say that he would run the risk and go into such dangerous places, when he can live comfortably as he does here, and never have to do with any wicked men again?"

Then Silvio looked at Rico, and said, "Will you go to fetch Stineli, Rico, or not?"

"Yes; I will," said Rico firmly.

"Oh, merciful heavens! now Rico is getting unmanageable too," cried the mother, quite horrified. "And now I do not know what to do. Take your fiddle, Rico, and play something, and sing; I must go into the garden." And the good woman ran quickly forth into the garden under the fig-trees, for she thought that her little son would forget the thing more quickly if he had not a chance to talk to her about it.

But the two good friends within neither played nor sang, but excited each other almost to fever point with all kinds of representations of how Stineli should be brought there, and of what would happen afterwards when she had fairly arrived. Rico utterly forgot to take his leave, although it was quite dark; and Mrs. Menotti purposely remained in the garden, thinking that Silvio would soon fall asleep. At last, however, she did come in, and Rico took his departure at once; but she had a bad time of it with Silvio, after all. He positively would not close his eyes until his mother promised that Rico should go to fetch Stineli; but she could not make any such promise, and the little fellow did not cease insisting until his mother said, "Be quiet, now; the night will set every thing straight." For she thought in the night he will forget his notion, as had often been the case, and he will have some other fancy.

At last the child was quiet and slept; but his mother had miscalculated the affair. Scarcely was it dawn when the little fellow called out from his bed, "Is every thing set straight now, mother?"

As it was impossible for her to reply in the affirmative to this question, the storm broke out again, and a more violent one than she had ever experienced before with her little boy, and lasted through the whole day quite late into the evening; and on the following day the same thing recommenced.

Silvio had never been so persistent in any fancy before. When he screamed and cried she was able to bear it; but when the hours of pain and suffering came, and the child went on whining and complaining in the most touching manner, saying,

"One only feels perfectly well with Stineli, and nowhere else," that cut his mother to the heart, and seemed like a reproach to her, as if she would not do something that might make him well again; but how could she possibly even think of it?

She had heard herself Rico's answer to Silvio when he asked if he knew how to go to Stineli. It was,--

"No, I do not know the way; but I can easily find one."

She went on hoping day after day that Silvio would take up some new whim, as had always before been the case: she had never found it otherwise. If he had wished for something when he was well, he had always given it up when his pain came on. But it was quite different this time, and there really was a reason too. Rico's stories and remarks about his friend Stineli had taken firm possession of the mind of the over-sensitive child; and he believed that nothing would hurt him again, if she were only by his side. So Silvio went on day after day in increasing distress; and his mother did not know where to turn for counsel and support.

CHAPTER XVI.
COUNSEL THAT BRINGS JOY TO MANY.

In all this trouble and uncertainty it was a real comfort to Mrs. Menotti to see the long black coat of the kind-hearted old priest, who had not been to visit her for a long time, coming through the garden gate.

She sprang up from her seat, crying out joyfully, "Look, Silvio; there comes the dear, good priest!" and went towards him. But Silvio, in his anger over every thing, said, as loud as he could, "I would rather it were Stineli!"

Then he crept quickly under the coverlet, so that the priest need not know where the voice came from. His mother, however, was dreadfully shocked, and begged the good man, who now entered the room, not to take offence at this greeting, as it was not really so bad as it sounded.

Silvio did not stir, but said softly, under the bed-cover,--

"I really mean just what I say."

The father must have had a suspicion of where the voice came from. He stepped at once to the bedside; and, though there was not a hair of Silvio's head even to be seen, he said, "God bless you, my son! how are you? How is your health nowadays? and why do you creep into this hidden hole like a little badger? Come out, and explain it all to me. What do you mean by Stineli?"

Now Silvio crept forth, for he had the priest in great respect now that he was so close to him. He stretched out his little thin hand in greeting, and said, "Rico's Stineli, I mean."

His mother now interposed with the explanation, for the father shook his head very doubtfully as he seated himself by the bedside. The good woman related the whole affair about Stineli, and told how her little boy had got the idea firmly fixed in his noddle that he would never be well again unless this Stineli could come to him; and how even Rico had become unreasonable, and declared that he could go to fetch Stineli, even though he did not know a single stock nor stone of the way; and it was such a long journey up into the mountains, moreover, and it was impossible to realize what horrible people they were who lived up there. But it proved how very bad they must be when a tender little fellow like Rico preferred to incur the great danger of the journey than to remain among such rude folk. "If it were practicable," however, added Mrs. Menotti, "no money would seem to me wasted that would procure me such a girl to quiet Silvio's longing, and to have some one to help take care of him;" for sometimes she had almost too much to endure, and felt as if she must give up altogether. And Rico, who was usually very discreet in his conversation, was of the opinion that nobody could help her so much nor so well in every way as this same Stineli. He ought to know her very well, too; and certainly, if she really corresponded to his description, it would be a great escape for such a girl to get away from the mountains; but she did not know of anybody who would do them such a favor as to bring her.

To all this discourse the kind priest lent an attentive ear in profound silence, until Mrs. Menotti had quite finished. Indeed, he could not have got a word in edgewise if he had been inclined; for the good woman had not opened her heart for a long time, and it was so full that it almost choked her when she gave her words full expression, and she quite lost her breath.

Now quiet reigned for a while, then the good man began very calmly to smoke his second pipe; and presently he said, "H--m, h--m, Mrs. Menotti; I rather think you have an impression of the mountaineers that is decidedly exaggerated. There are good Christians there as elsewhere; and now that there are so many ways of doing things discovered, it would be also quite possible to get up there without danger. We must bethink ourselves about that, and find out about it."

After this opinion, the priest stopped to refresh himself a little from his snuff-box; then he went on:--

"There are all sorts of trades-people who are always coming down to Bergamo,--sheep and horse dealers: they know the road well enough, of course. We can obtain information, and then bethink ourselves: we can find a way sooner or later. If you are in earnest about it, Mrs. Menotti, I will look about a little. I go every year once or twice to Bergamo, and I will take the thing in hand for you."

Mrs. Menotti was so filled with gratitude at this promise, that words utterly failed her that were, in her opinion, adequate to express her thanks. Suddenly all the heavy thoughts had vanished that had oppressed her day and night for such a long time past, and in which she was getting more and more involved the more she puzzled over them, so that at the last she saw no hope of a decision. Now the Father took the whole burden upon himself, and she could refer her troublesome little Silvio to him.

While this conference was taking place, the little invalid had almost pierced the priest through with his great gray eyes, so great was his interest in what they said. When the priest arose, and held his hand towards the child to say good-by, the little thin fingers were pressed into his big palm as if he were making a firm contract.

The father gave his promise to bring tidings as soon as he had obtained the necessary information; and then they could decide whether the thing could be done, or whether Silvio must give up his wish altogether.

Week after week slipped by, but Silvio did not waver. He had a firm ground of hope now by which to hold; and, moreover, Rico had become so lively and amusing, that he was hardly to be recognized. It acted upon him like a spark that kindled a joyful bonfire when he learned the priest's comforting words; and a new life was awakened in the lad. He knew more stories to tell Silvio than ever before; and when he took his fiddle in his hand, he produced such heart-stirring tones and tunes, that Mrs. Menotti could not tear herself from the room where the boys were, and was full of astonishment at Rico's store of music.

It was only in this room at Mrs. Menotti's that Rico fully enjoyed his instrument. It sounded so well in the large, lofty space, where it was quiet and peaceful, without a taint of tobacco-smoke, or the clamor of noisy men; and he was not confined to dance music, but at liberty to play as his fancy directed. Every day he went with increasing pleasure to Mrs. Menotti's, and often said to himself, as he entered, "This is the way it must feel when one is entering his own home."

But it was not his home: he only was permitted to go there for a little while, and away again.

There had come over Rico a very decided change within a short time; and the landlady, who perceived it clearly, was greatly perplexed thereby. When she placed a nasty broken pail of refuse before him, saying, "There, Rico, carry this to the hens," he would step aside a little, put his hands behind his back, to show that he did not mean to touch the pail, and say quietly, "I prefer that some one else should do that;" and when she brought out an old pair of shoes and handed them to him to carry to the cobbler, he did the same, saying. "I prefer that you should give them to another person to carry."

Now the landlady was a clever woman, and knew how to put two and two together; and it had not escaped her that Rico was quite another person within a short time, and looked very differently too. Mrs. Menotti had always dressed him very nicely since she had undertaken that office; but when she observed how well his clothes became him, and what an air of real gentility he had, she used finer materials than at first; and the lad always took good care of his person and his dress, for he detested uncleanliness and disorder, both on his own appearance and in his surroundings. All of this was not unnoticed, nor did she ever forget that even as Rico had poured out his pocketful of gold upon the table before her after his first "dance evening," so had he continued to do faithfully, and not so much as looked as if he would like to keep one bit for himself.

He brought more and more each time; for it was not only for his dance music that he was called so often, but because of his songs, that were very popular.

And the landlady recognized that it was her best policy to treat him always kindly and well; and she did not trouble him about the hens nor the shoes, and required such little services from him no more.

It was now three years since Rico made his first entry into Peschiera. He was now a tall, fourteen-year old stripling, and whoever laid eyes upon him found him pleasing to look upon.

Once again the golden sun of autumn burnished the surface of the Lake of Garda, and the heavens lay blue above the tranquil waves. In the garden the great bunches of grapes hung gold against the trellises, and the red flowers of the oleander glistened in the sunbeams.

It was quiet in Silvio's room, for his mother was without in the garden gathering grapes and figs for the evening. The invalid lay listening for Rico's step, for this was the time of his usual visit. The wicket opened: Silvio pulled himself up in his bed. A long black coat came slowly toward the door,--it was the priest. Silvio did not think of hiding himself this time. He stretched out his little arm as far as he was able, to shake hands with the good man, before he had fairly entered the room.

This welcome pleased the priest, who walked at once into the room, and to the child's bedside, even though he saw Mrs. Menotti's form behind him in the garden.

"This is right, my son," he said. "And how do you find yourself?"

"All right," said Silvio quickly; and, looking eagerly at the good man, he added softly, "When may Rico go?"

Seating himself by the bedside, the good man said, a little pompously, "To-morrow, at five o'clock, Rico will start, my son."

Mrs. Menotti entered as he was speaking, and it was with some difficulty that the priest could quiet her enough to get a chance to tell his story in a consecutive way, and to make himself understood; and all the time he was speaking, Silvio's eyes were fixed upon his face like a little sparrow-hawk.

He had come directly from Bergamo, where he had passed two days. He had made all the necessary arrangements with a horse-trader,--a friend of his who had been travelling, for thirty years or more, every autumn, and knew the way over the mountains that Rico must take. He knew, also, how the journey could be made without leaving the coach, or sleeping by the way. He was going there himself, and would take Rico under his charge, if the lad would go to Bergamo by the early train. The man knew all the drivers and conductors, also; and would arrange for his and his companion's return, and recommend them so well that there would be no trouble or danger.

The Father was convinced that there was no hindrance to Rico's going in perfect safety, and gave his blessing to the undertaking.

As he stood by the garden-hedge, after saying good-by to Silvio, Mrs. Menotti, who had accompanied him thus far, detained him for a moment, to ask again, full of sudden anxiety, "Oh, there will not be any danger to his life, I hope? Nor that he may lose his way, and go wandering about in the mountains? You do not think that possible, do you, Father?" But the good man quieted her fears; and she returned to the house, thinking of what there remained to do for Rico, who entered the garden at this moment, and was greeted by such a startling cry of joy from Silvio, that he reached the bedside in three leaps to find out what it all meant.

"What is the matter? What ails you?" Rico kept asking; and Silvio repeated, "I will tell you, I will tell you!" until, in real anxiety, his mother came to his aid. Soon, however, she left the boys to enjoy their happiness together; and went about her business, which she thought very important. She fetched a portmanteau, and placed a huge piece of smoked meat first of all at the bottom, then a half loaf of bread, a big parcel of preserved plums and figs, and a bottle of wine, carefully wrapped in a cloth. Then came the clothes,--two shirts and a pair of shoes, two pair of stockings, and pocket-handkerchiefs; for it seemed always to Mrs. Menotti as if Rico were going to the farthermost part of the world; and she only now fully realized how dearly she loved the lad, for she felt that she could not get on without him.

All the while, as she was packing, she would pause, sit down, and say to herself, anxiously, "Oh, I do hope there will not be an accident!"

Presently she brought the portmanteau down-stairs, and counselled Rico to go at once and explain to the landlady how every thing had happened; and to ask if she would allow him to go, and not oppose it; and afterwards Rico was to carry the portmanteau to the station.

The boy was in the greatest surprise over his portmanteau. He obeyed in silence, as usual, however, and went to the landlady. He explained to her that he was going back to the mountains to bring Stineli back with him, and that the priest had arranged it so that he was to start on the following morning at five o'clock.

It produced a feeling of respect at once in the mind of the landlady when she found that the priest was at the head of the business. But she naturally wished to know who this Stineli might be, and what the idea was in fetching her; for she hoped it might be on her account.

She only found out that Stineli was a girl whose name was Stineli, and that she was coming to Mrs. Menotti. So she let the thing go; for she would not interfere, for the world, with that lady's wishes. She was only too glad that Rico had been left to her for so long. She took it for granted that Stineli was Rico's sister, only that he had not said so, because he never did say any thing about his family.

So she told all the guests in the inn that evening that Rico was going to bring his sister down to Peschiera, because he had found out how well they all lived there.

In order to show how highly she held the lad in respect, she had a big basket brought down from the attic, and filled it with sausages and cheese, and slices of bread, and eggs, saying,--

"You must not get hungry on the way; and what is left over, you can eat while you are there. It will not be too much; and coming back, you will need something too. You are certainly coming back, Rico, are you not?"

"Certainly," replied the lad. "In eight days I shall be back again."

In Mrs. Menotti's hands he placed his beloved fiddle, for he would not have trusted it to any one else; and then he took his leave for eight days, for he could easily be back again in that time, if every thing went well.

CHAPTER XVII.
BACK AGAIN OVER THE MOUNTAINS.

Full of impatience, Rico stood at the station long before the appointed time, and could scarcely be quiet while waiting for the train. Again he took his seat in the carriage, as he had done three years before, but not now crouched timidly in a corner with his violin in his hand. He took a whole seat for himself this time; for he placed his portmanteau and his basket next him, and they took up a deal of room. He met the horse-dealer in Bergamo without difficulty, and they travelled along in the same carriage together, and then across the lake. When they left the boat they went towards the inn, where the big post-wagon stood with the horses already harnessed. It all came back to Rico's memory with great distinctness,--how he had stood there in the night, quite alone, after the students had all gone their ways; and opposite he espied the stable-door where he had seen the lantern hanging, and had found the friendly sheep-dealer again. It was evening now; and they took their places at once in the coach, and went towards the mountain. Rico sat within, this time, with his companion, and had scarcely settled himself comfortably in his corner when his eyes closed and he slept; for he had not slept an hour on the preceding night, so great had been his excitement. Now he made it up, without once awakening, until the sun stood high in the heavens, and the coach moved very slowly; and when he stuck his head out of the window, he saw, to his utter astonishment, that they were ascending the zigzag road up the Maloja, that was so familiar to him from his childhood.

He could not see much from the window,--only a turning in the road now and then; but now he did want to see everything that lay about them. At last the coach stopped: they had reached the summit. There was the inn, there the spot where he had sat and talked with the driver. All the passengers got out for a moment, and the horses were fed. Rico also descended, and asked very humbly of the driver if he might be allowed to take a seat on the box with him.

"Will you let me climb up there, and ride as far as Sils?" he asked.

"Up with you!" said the coachman. They all took their places, and merrily rolled the coach down the smooth road and along the level way. Now they reached the lake. Yonder lay the wooded peninsula, and there the white houses of Sils, and beyond was Sils Maria. The little church shone in the morning sunshine, and over towards the mountain were two cottages. Rico's heart began to beat wildly. Where was Stineli? A few steps farther, and the coach stood still in Sils.

Stineli had suffered a great deal since her friend's disappearance. The children were larger, and the work ever increasing; and the greater part fell to her share, for she was the eldest of the children, and the youngest of the rest of the family; so the cry was always, "Stineli can do this: she is old enough now;" and presently, "Stineli must look after that, she is so young." She had no one with whom to share her pleasures since Rico's departure, even if she had a moment to herself.

Her good grandmother had died the year before, and from that time forward the girl had no relaxation whatever; but from morning to evening there was nothing but incessant toil.

She never lost heart, however, although she had wept bitterly over the loss of her grandmother; and every day the thought arose several times in her mind, without her good grandmother and Rico the world was no longer as beautiful as formerly.

On a sunny Saturday morning she came out of the stable with a big bundle of straw poised on her head. She meant to weave some nice brushes, for the evening sweeping. The sun was shining all down the pathway towards Sils, and she stood gazing in that direction. An unknown lad came along the road,--certainly no Silser, she thought; and yet as he drew near he stood still and looked at her, and she returned his gaze, and was much perplexed. In an instant, however, away went her bundle of straw, and she rushed forward towards the motionless figure before her, crying out,--

'O Rico! are you still alive? Have you come back again? But how big you are, Rico! I did not know you, at first; but as soon as I saw your face, then I was sure,-- nobody has a face like yours."

So Stineli stood with glowing cheeks before the lad; and he grew as white as chalk from excitement, and could not find words to speak his joy, but looked and looked at the girl. Presently he said,--

"You have grown, too, Stineli, but are not otherwise changed. The nearer I came to the house, the more anxious I got lest you might be altered."

"Oh, to think that you are really here, Rico!" cried Stineli, joyfully. "Oh, if the grandmother only knew! But come in, Rico; they will all be surprised." She ran on before to open the door, and Rico followed.

The children hid themselves one behind the other; and their mother rose and greeted the lad as if he were a stranger, and asked what his wishes were. Neither she nor the children had an idea who he was. Now Trudi and Sami came into the room, and bowed to him as they passed through. "Does not one of you know him?" said Stineli, at last. "Don't you see it is Rico?"

They were astonished and full of their surprise when their father came to his dinner. Rico advanced towards him, offering his hand, which the man took, but looked steadily at the strange lad.

"Is it some kind of a relation?" he asked; for he was never very sure about the members of the family who sometimes visited them.

"Even the father does not know him," said Stineli, rather vexed.

"Why, it is Rico, father!"

"Well, well: that is good," remarked he; and looked the lad well over from head to foot this time, adding,--

"You need not be ashamed to show yourself. Have you learned some sort of a trade? Let us all be seated, and then you can tell us what has happened to you."

But Rico did not sit down at once: he kept looking towards the doorway. At last he asked, hesitatingly,--

"Where is the grandmother?"

"She lies over there in Sils, not far from the old schoolmaster," was the reply. Rico had hesitated with his question, for he feared this would be the answer; he had noticed the grandmother's absence at once. He took his seat with the others at the table, but was silent for a while, and could not eat a morsel: he had loved the grandmother dearly. However, the father wanted to hear his story, and to know what had become of him on the day they all searched for him in the ravines, and what he had seen and done in the world. So the boy told all his story, and about Mrs. Menotti and Silvio; and explained distinctly that he wished to take Stineli back with him to Peschiera, if her parents would consent. Stineli made very big eyes while her friend was talking: she had not lost one word of his history. Her heart was as if on fire with joy. To go to Rico's beautiful lake with him, to live with Mrs. Menotti and her sick son, who was so anxious for her to come,--that would be happiness indeed!

There was a long silence after this. Stineli's father never decided hastily. At last he said, "It is true that when one goes among strangers there is much to be learned; but I cannot let Stineli go,--there can be no question of that. She is needed here at home; but one of the others may go,--Trudi, perhaps."

"Yes, yes: that will do," said the mother. "I cannot get along without Stineli."

Then Trudi raised her head from her plate, and said, "That suits me very well. There is nothing but children's racket here at home."

Stineli did not speak. She only looked anxiously towards Rico, wondering if he would not say any thing more since her father seemed so decided, and whether he would take Trudi with him as proposed. The lad, however, looked calmly at her father, saying, "No: that won't do at all. It is precisely Stineli whom the sick boy Silvio wishes, and nobody else; and he knows very well what he wants. He would only send Trudi home again, and she would have taken the journey for nothing. Mrs. Menotti told me to say, that if Stineli got on well with her son, she would give her every month five gulden to send home to her family, if they cared for it; and I am sure that Stineli and Silvio will agree famously,--just as sure as if I saw it with my own eyes now," added the lad.

Pushing his plate to one side, Stineli's father put his cap on his head. He had finished his dinner; and when he had some very severe thinking to do, he was always more comfortable with his cap on. It seemed to help him to collect his thoughts.

He thought, always in silence, how much labor he would have to perform before he could earn even one good gulden; and he said to himself, "Five gulden every month without lifting a finger."

So he shoved his cap first on one side and then on the other; and said, at last, "She may go. One of the others can do the work in the house."

Stineli's eyes sparkled, but the mother looked sadly at all the little heads and plates. Who would keep them all nice and in order?

But the father's cap got another shove. Something else had occurred to him.

"Stineli has not yet been confirmed, and ought to be before she goes away."

"I am not to be confirmed for two years yet, father," said the girl eagerly; "so that I can go away for two years perfectly well, and come back quite in time for that."

This was a good decision, and everybody was satisfied. The father and mother thought, even if every thing does go badly without Stineli, it will only be for a while; and when she comes back again, all will be well. And Trudi thought, "Just as soon as she comes back again, I will go and then we shall see if I come back."

But Rico and Stineli merely glanced at each other, and laughed with their eyes for pure joy.

As the father looked upon the affair as settled, he rose from the table, saying, "She may go to-morrow: then we shall know where we stand."

Her mother, on the contrary, objected to this, saying that it could not be managed so quickly, and complained bitterly, until her father gave in, and said she should go the following Monday, and would not hear of a later date; for he thought that there would be a continual fuss until the departures were fairly over.

Work there was now for Stineli in abundance. Rico understood that this must be the case, and he addressed himself to Sami, and said he would like to see whether every thing remained as formerly in Sils-Maria; and that he had a sack and a basket to fetch from Sils, and perhaps Sami would go with him to help him; so they went forth.

Firstly, Rico paused before his former home, and gazed at the old house-door and the hen-house. It was just as it had been. He asked Sami who lived there now,--if his cousin were there, and alone.

But he heard that the cousin had long ago gone away towards Silvaplana, and nobody knew any thing about her; for she had not shown her face in Sils-Maria again.

There were people living in the house, about whom Rico knew nothing. Everywhere that he went with Sami, from the old well-known houses and stables the people stared at him as if he were an utter stranger; not one of them recognized him in the least.

As he crossed over, towards evening, to Sils, he turned aside a little towards the churchyard. He wanted to see the grave where the old grandmother was buried; but Sami did not rightly know where she lay.

They returned home just as it was growing dark, laden with basket and portmanteau. Stineli stood at the well, and brushed out the stable buckets for the last time; and as Rico stood there by her side, she said, flushed with pleasure, and with her exertions over the pails, "I can scarcely believe that it is true, Rico."

"But I do," said he so decidedly, that the girl looked at him surprised. "But of course, Stineli," he added, "you have not been thinking it out this long time as I have."

There was a change in Rico that the girl noticed at once. Formerly he would not have spoken in this firm and decided manner.

They had arranged a bed for Rico up in the room under the roof. He carried his things up there, and meant to open them the following morning.

When they were all seated the next day at table,--a beautiful, clear Sunday morning,--down came Rico, and poured out before Urschli and Peterli a big heap of plums and figs. The latter fruit they had never seen at all; and the plums were finer than any that they were accustomed to; and his sausages and meat and eggs he placed in the middle of the table. As soon as their admiration and surprise had a little subsided, they all fell to and ate with a wonderful relish, and the children were munching the sweet figs quite late into the evening.

CHAPTER XVIII.
TWO HAPPY TRAVELLERS.

On Monday evening the journey was to begin. The horse-dealer had impressed this fact so thoroughly on Rico's memory, that there was not a chance for a mistake. After the farewells were all said, Rico and Stineli went towards Sils together, while her mother, with all the little children clustered about her, stood upon the doorstep and looked after them.

Sami accompanied them to carry the portmanteau on his head, and Rico carried the basket on one side, and Stineli held it on the other. Stineli's clothes had just filled it.

When they reached the church in Sils, Stineli said, "Oh, if my grandmother could only see us now! We will go to say good-by to her, Rico." He was very willing, and told Stineli how he had already tried to find the grave, but had not succeeded.

The girl was better informed than her brother.

When the post-wagon came along and stopped, the driver called out, "Are the couple ready who are to go down to the Lake of Garda? I was asking for them yesterday."

The horse-dealer had given them a good recommendation; and the driver called out that they should climb up to the top: the others had found it too cold. "You are younger," he said.

So saying, he helped them up to the seats behind the box, and took out a thick horse-blanket, and wrapped them up snugly therein; and off they went.

For the first time since they had come together again, the two young people were alone, and could talk freely and undisturbed, and tell each other how they had passed the three long years since they parted. And they chattered away happily under the starry heavens, never thinking of sleep in their joy at being together.

Towards morning they reached the lake, and arrived in Peschiera at the same hour as Rico had before arrived, and walked along the road to the lake-side. But Rico did not wish his companion to see the lake until she had reached the spot he called his own; so he led her through the trees until they came to the little stone bridge in the open.

There lay the lake in the light of the setting sun; and the children sat side by side on the little mound, and gazed across the water.

There it was, just as Rico had described it, but more, much more lovely; for such colors Stineli had never seen before.

She looked about her towards the purple mountains, across the golden waters, and she cried out with all her heart, "Yes, it is finer than the Lake of Sils."

But Rico felt that it had never yet been so exquisitely beautiful as on this evening when he and Stineli saw it together.

Rico had another secret joy that he cherished in his heart. How surprised Silvio and his mother would be to see them! Nobody had expected them back so soon. Nobody would look for them before the end of the week, and now there they sat by the lake-side.

They did not quit the little mound until the sun had fairly disappeared.

Rico pointed out to his companion the spot where his mother stood washing something in the lake, and how he used to sit waiting until she had finished; and then he told how they walked back together, hand in hand, over the little bridge.

"But where did you go when you went back?" asked Stineli. "Have you never found the house that you returned to?"

Rico could not say. "When I go up there, away from the lake towards the railroad, I seem to remember that there I stood with my mother, or sat with her upon a garden-seat with the red flowers before us; but now nothing is to be seen like the house, and I do not even recognize the road at all."

At last they arose, and went towards the garden. Rico carried the portmanteau, and the girl the basket. As they entered the garden, Stineli called out too loud, in her delight, "Oh, the beautiful, beautiful flowers!"

Silvio heard these unfortunate words, and pulled himself up in an instant, crying out, at the top of his lungs,--

"Here comes Rico with his Stineli!"

His poor mother thought that he had an attack of fever. She thrust her things back into the chest which she was arranging,--every thing in again, pell-mell,--and ran quickly to the bedside.

At that moment Rico walked boldly into the room, and the good woman almost fell over backward in her surprise and delight; for until that very instant she had secretly been a prey to the darkest fears, always believing that Rico's adventure would cost him his life.

A maiden came behind Rico, with a friendly face that won Mrs. Menotti's heart in a twinkling, for she was a very impressionable woman.

First of all, however, she shook Rico's hands almost off in her welcoming grasp; and in the meantime Stineli had gone over to the bedside and placed her arm about the thin shoulders of the child, and smiled into his face as if they were old and dear friends, while Silvio in return put his arm about her neck, and drew her face down to his.

Straightway Stineli placed a present for the child before him. She had put it conveniently in her pocket, so that she could place her hand on it at once. It was a toy that had been Peterli's favorite before any other,--a pine-cone, with a thin wire introduced into each little opening between the hard scales, and a little figure, made of sole-leather, perched on the top of each bit of wire. All these tiny figures shook and nodded so merrily towards each other, and had such funnily painted little faces, that Silvio could scarcely stop laughing at them.

Mrs. Menotti had learned from Rico all that he had to tell her of importance while this play went on,--for she was anxious to learn from himself that all had gone quietly and safely,--then she turned to the girl, and greeted her with heartfelt kindness; and Stineli made answer more with her kindly eyes than with her tongue, for she could not speak a word of Italian, and had to help herself out with such Romanish words as she had learned.

But she was quick-witted, and found a way to make herself understood without difficulty; for, if the right word was wanting, she described the thing cleverly with her fingers, and by all sorts of signs, which amused Silvio exceedingly; for it was a kind of game of guessing for him all the time.

Now Mrs. Menotti went over to the cupboard, where all the service for the table was kept, and brought out tablecloth and plates, cold chicken, fruit, and wine; which, when Stineli observed, she hastened after her to aid her, and did it so neatly and handily that there remained little for Mrs. Menotti to do; and she stood gazing at the nimble, willing girl, who had soon served Silvio also, as he lay in bed, cutting his food for him, and helping him neatly and rapidly, which pleased the child very much.

Mrs. Menotti seated herself, saying, "I have not had such help as this in many a year; but, come now, Stineli: sit down, and eat with us."

And they sat and chatted and ate together, as if they were old friends who had always been accustomed to such free intercourse.

Rico began to give an account of the journey after they had finished eating, and Stineli meanwhile quietly replaced every thing in the cupboard; for she knew well enough, without being told, how such work should be done. Then she seated herself by Silvio's bedside, and made shadow pictures on the wall with her supple fingers; and Silvio laughed aloud, and called the names,--"A hare! A beast with horns! A spider with long legs!"

So sped away the first evening quickly and merrily, and they all were taken by surprise when it struck ten o'clock. Rico rose, for he knew he must be going; but a dark cloud came over his countenance.

He said shortly, "Good-night," and went away. But the girl ran after him; and in the garden she took his hand, saying, "Now you must not be sad, Rico, it *is* so beautiful here. I cannot tell you how lovely I find it, nor how happy I am; and I owe it all, all to you. And you will come again to-morrow, and every day, will you not, Rico?"

"Yes," he said; and looked at Stineli with a most melancholy expression. "Yes; and every evening, when it is most beautiful, I must be off and away, because I belong to nobody."

'Oh! do not think in that way, Rico," said his friend encouragingly. "Have we not always belonged to each other, and have not I often rejoiced over that thought all these three years that are past? And when things were almost unsupportable, and I longed to get away, have not I always said to myself, 'If I could only be with Rico again, I would bear any thing?' And now it has come about as we wished, and, indeed, far better than I had imagined; and will you not be happy with me, Rico?"

"Yes; that I will," said the lad; and his countenance cleared a little.

He did belong to somebody, after all; and Stineli's words had restored his tranquility. They shook hands again; and Rico went through the garden-gate, and away.

When Stineli returned to the room, and, by Mrs. Menotti's directions, was about to say good-night to Silvio, the child began to dispute again, and declared that he would not be separated from his newly-found friend even for a few hours; but would have her sit by his bedside all night long, and say funny words to him, and look at him with her laughing eyes.

Nothing that his mother could say produced any impression upon him, until she spoke thus: "Very well; if you keep Stineli standing by your bed to amuse you all night, she will soon be as ill as you are, and not be able to get up at all, but have to lie in bed, and you will not see her for a long time."

So, after a while, the child released his hold of Stineli's arm, and said,--

"There, go to sleep; but come to me again to-morrow early."

This was promised; and Mrs. Menotti showed the girl into a neat little bedroom that looked out upon the garden, whence a delicious scent of flowers rose through the open window.

With every day that passed Stineli became more and more necessary to little Silvio. If she only went out-of-doors for a few moments, he considered it a misfortune. He was obedient and quiet enough, however, when she stayed with him; and did every thing she bade him do, and did not tease his mother as before.

And it seemed as if the nervous little fellow had less frequent attacks of pain since Stineli's arrival. Indeed, he had not complained since her coming, and she had been with them many days.

It must certainly be acknowledged that she was the most amusing of companions, and turned every thing that came in her way into a game. She had always lived with children, and constantly had their entertainment in her mind. She had also learned a great many words from Silvio, and could soon chatter away with him at her ease; and when she did get the words twisted and upside down, it was even more funny, and Silvio looked upon that as a game made expressly for him.

Mrs. Menotti never saw Rico entering the garden but she ran towards him, for now she was at liberty to move about freely; and she always drew him a little aside to tell him what a treasure he had brought into the house for her, how happy and gay her Silvio had become, and that she never would have believed that such a girl as Stineli existed on the face of the earth; for with Silvio she was as merry as if her only pleasure consisted in playing the little games he liked, while she was as wise and intelligent as any grown woman with Mrs. Menotti, and understood housework so that it all seemed to go on of its own accord; and nicely, too, as if every day were Sunday. In short, Mrs. Menotti could not find words enough to praise Stineli in all the ways in which she found her admirable; and Rico was always happy in listening to these praises.

When they all sat together in the pleasant room, and exchanged loving and happy glances, they felt that they never wanted to be separated, and called themselves the happiest family in the whole world, and needed for nothing.

But the clouds on Rico's brow grew dark as night came on, and towards ten o'clock every thing looked black and blacker; and even if Mrs. Menotti, in her contentment, did not notice it, Stineli did, and secretly worried over it, thinking, "It is just as if there were a thunder-storm in the air."

CHAPTER XIX.
CLOUDS ON THE BEAUTIFUL LAKE OF GARDA.

It was a beautiful Sunday in autumn, and across the Lake of Riva there was to be a "dance evening," and Rico was to go over there to play; so he would not be able to pass the day with Stineli and the rest. They talked this over and over through the week, for it was a great trial to them all when Rico did not come for Sunday; and Stineli tried to find all sorts of little reasons to reconcile Rico, and to make the affair seem less unpleasant.

"You will go across the lake in the sunlight, and return under the beautiful stars; and we shall be thinking of you the whole time," she said to him, when he first mentioned that he should be away on Sunday.

On Saturday evening Rico brought his violin, for Stineli's greatest pleasure was to hear him play. The lad played lovely tunes one after another; but they were all sad melodies, and seemed to make him sadder still, for he looked down at his instrument with a kind of indignant sorrow, as if it did him a real injury.

Suddenly he pushed it away from him, long before the clock had struck ten, and said, "I am going away."

Mrs. Menotti tried to detain him; she could not understand what was amiss. Stineli had looked steadily at him while he was playing. Now she said, quietly,--

"I will go with you a little way."

"No," cried Silvio; "do not go. Stay here with me."

"Yes, yes, Stineli!" said Rico. "Stay here, and let me go alone."

And, saying this, he looked at his friend exactly as he had looked when he came away from the schoolmaster's house, and joined Stineli at the wood-pile, so long ago, saying then, "It is all of no use!"

Stineli went to Silvio's bedside, and said softly, "Be a good boy, Silvio; and to-morrow I will tell you the very prettiest and drollest story about Peterli; but now do not make a noise."

Silvio really did keep quiet, and Stineli went after Rico. When they reached the hedge, Rico turned about, and pointed towards the brightly lighted window that looked so pleasant and friendly from the garden, and said, "Go back there, Stineli. You belong there, and there you are at home; but I belong in the streets. I am a homeless fellow, and shall always be so: now let me go away."

"No, no; I will not let you go in this mood, Rico. Where do you mean to go?"

"To the lake," said the young man; and went towards the bridge. As they stood together on the little mound, they were silent for a while, listening to the murmur of the waves. At last, Rico said,--

"Do you understand, if you were not here, I would go away at once, far away?--but I do not know where I should go. Wherever I go, I shall be homeless, and have to be fiddling forever in public-houses where they are noisy, just as if they had lost their senses, and I must always sleep in a room in which I dislike to be; but you belong to them there in that beautiful house, and I do not belong anywhere. And I tell you, Stineli, when I look down there, I think if my mother had only cast me to the waves before she died, then I should not have been this homeless wanderer."

With ever-increasing trouble, Stineli listened to these words of her friend; but when he pronounced these last, she became really alarmed, and said hastily, "O Rico! you ought not to say such things. I am sure that you have not said 'Our Father' for a long, long time; and these wicked thoughts are the consequence."

"No: I have not prayed for a long time," said Rico. "I have forgotten how."

These words gave his companion a severe shock.

"Oh, dear! what would my grandmother say to this, Rico?" she cried, in distress. "She would be in sad trouble about you. Do not you remember how she told us, 'He who forgets his Lord's Prayer is sure to get into trouble?' Rico, you must learn it again. I will teach it to you this minute: it will not take you long."

And the good girl began, with pious zeal, and repeated the prayer twice or thrice over to her friend; and, while she thus emphasized the words, she noticed that there was a great deal of especial comfort for Rico contained therein; and, as she ended, she said,--

"Do not you see, Rico, if all the kingdom belongs to the good God, He can surely find you a home? for He has all the power, so He can give it to you if He chooses."

"Now you can plainly see, Stineli," replied the youth, "if the good God has a home for me in His kingdom, and has the power to give it to me, and does not, it is because He does **not** choose to."

"Yes; but you forget something," continued Stineli. "The good God may say, 'If Rico wants any thing from me, he should pray to me.'"

In reply to this, Rico had no answer. He remained silent for some time; then he said, "Repeat the Lord's Prayer again, Stineli: I will learn it."

His companion gladly complied, and it was soon learned. Then they separated, and each went home; but Rico's thoughts were busy with the "kingdom and the power."

Once more in his quiet room, he prayed humbly, and with a softened heart; for he felt that he had been in the wrong to believe that the good God ought to give him what he wished for, when he did not even remember to pray to Him.

Stineli returned to the garden very full of anxious thought. She turned over and over in her mind whether she ought to tell all this to Mrs. Menotti. Perhaps she might be able to find some other employment for Rico than this fiddling in the public-houses for dancing, that was so detestable to the lad. But the thought of troubling Mrs. Menotti with her affairs passed quickly from her mind as she entered the room again.

Silvio lay upon his pillows with flushed cheeks, breathing heavily and irregularly; and by the bedside sat his mother, and wept.

The little invalid had had another of his severe attacks, and a little anger at Stineli's absence had increased the fever. His mother was so cast down, that she did not seem to Stineli the same person at all. When she, at last, recovered her spirits a little, she said,--

"Come here, Stineli. Sit down here by my side: I want to tell you something.

"I have something that lies very heavily at my heart; so heavily, that sometimes it seems to me that I cannot bear it any longer. It is true you are young, but you are so sensible, and have seen a great deal; and it seems to me that I should be relieved if I could talk it over with you.

"You see how Silvio suffers, and how ill he is,--my only son. Now I have not only the distress of his sickness, which can never be healed, but I often feel that perhaps it is a punishment from God, because I am holding and enjoying an unlawful property: although, to be sure, I did not seek to get it, and do not wish to keep it. But I will tell you every thing from the beginning.

"When we were married, Menotti and I,--he brought me over from Riva, where my father still lives,--Menotti had a very good friend living here, who was just about leaving, because the land had become hateful to him, owing to the death of his wife. This friend had a house--a little one--and large fields, though they were not very productive. He wanted my husband to take them all, and said that the land did not yield much; but if he would keep it all in good order, and the house also, that he would return to claim it in a few years.

"So the friends made their arrangements together, and said nothing about interest. My husband said, 'You will want to find every thing as it should be when you return;' for he meant to put it all in good condition, and understood the cultivating of land perfectly, which was thoroughly well known to his friend, who willingly left it all in his hands. But about one year later the railroad was built, and the little house had to come down, and the garden was taken too, with the fields, for the railway went right through them. So my husband got a great deal more money than they were really worth, and bought a far better piece of land and a garden, and built a house, all with the money; and the land produced fully twice what the other had, and we had most abundant harvests. I often said, 'It does not really belong to us, and we are living in luxury from the property of another. How I wish that we knew where he is!' But my husband quieted me, and said, 'I am keeping it all in order for him, and when he comes it is all his; and as to the profit that I have laid aside, he must have his share also.'

"Then Silvio was born; and when I discovered that the little fellow was ill, I kept saying over and over to my husband, 'We are living on property to which we have no right, and we are punished for it.' And sometimes it was so dreadful to me that poverty would have been more tolerable, and I would have gladly been homeless.

"My husband always tried to console me, and said, 'You will see how pleased he will be with me when he returns.' But he did not return. My husband died: it is now four years ago. Oh, what a life I have led since then! always thinking how can I be free from this unlawful property without doing any thing wrong, for it is my duty to keep it in good condition until our friend comes; and then I feared that he might be in misery somewhere while I am living so comfortably on his property, and know nothing of his whereabouts."

Stineli felt sincerely how much Mrs. Menotti was to be pitied; for she perfectly well understood her feeling, and how she was always reproaching herself for a thing that she could not change, and she comforted the good woman, saying,--

"When any one does not mean to do wrong, and means not to do wrong, then there is nothing but to trust to the good God and pray to Him for help; for He can turn our evil into His good, and He will do so when we are truly repentant over evil. I know all this from my grandmother's teaching; for once I was in great distress, and did not know what to do."

Then she told about Rico and the lake that he was always thinking of, and how she was the cause of his running away, and full of fear that it had cost him his life. But she said that she felt perfectly at ease after she had cast her burden on the Lord; and she advised Mrs. Menotti to do likewise, and assured her that she would derive the truest comfort from so doing. After this conversation Mrs. Menotti felt much relieved, and said they would all go to rest now, and thanked her young counsellor for her advice.

CHAPTER XX.
AT HOME.

One beautiful Sunday morning in autumn, Mrs. Menotti seated herself on the garden-bench in the midst of the glowing red flowers, and thoughtfully gazed about her,--now at the oleander and laurel bushes, now at the fig-trees laden with fruit, and again at the vines heavy with golden grapes; and she said, softly, "God knows I should be glad if I could lay aside this feeling of wrong-doing that weighs on my conscience, but certainly such a lovely spot as this one I could never find for a home."

Presently Rico came into the garden. He was obliged to go away in the afternoon; and he never passed a whole day without paying them a visit, if it were possible to do otherwise. As he was passing on towards Silvio's room, Mrs. Menotti called him.

"Come and sit down by me, Rico, for a moment. Who knows how long we may be able to stay in this place together?"

Rico was alarmed.

"Why do you say this, Mrs. Menotti? You do not think of going away, do you?"

Mrs. Menotti had to stop, for she could not tell him all her story. She remembered what Stineli had said to her the evening before about Rico. She was so full of her own thoughts at that time, that she did not fairly take in the import of her words. Now she began to wonder about it, the more she thought it over.

"Do tell me, Rico," she said, "were you ever here earlier?--I mean before; or what made you want to see the lake again, as Stineli told me was the case yesterday?"

"Yes; when I was little," said the lad. "Then I went away."

"How did you get here when you were little, Rico?"

"I was born here."

"What! here? What was your father, if he came here from the mountains yonder?"

"He did not come here from the mountains; only my mother did."

"Do I hear aright, Rico? Was your father born here?"

"Certainly. He was a native of this place."

"You never told me this before. This is wonderful. You have not a name like the people here. What was your father's name?"

"What was his name? It was Henrico Trevillo."

Mrs. Menotti sprang up from the seat as if she had had a shock.

"What did you say, Rico?" she cried out. "What did you say just now? Tell me again."

"I told you my father's name."

Mrs. Menotti was not listening: she ran towards the door.

"Stineli, bring me a kerchief," she cried. "I must go to the priest at once: I am trembling all over."

In great surprise, Stineli brought out the kerchief.

"Come with me a few steps, Rico," said the good woman, as she went through the garden. "I must ask you something more."

Rico had to repeat his father's name twice over; and when they had fairly reached the door of the priest's house, for a third time Mrs. Menotti asked,--

"What did you say it was? Are you quite sure?"

She hurried into the priest's house, and left Rico wondering what could have happened to put her into such a way.

Rico had brought his violin with him, for he knew that Stineli was particularly pleased to hear it. When he reached Silvio's room, he found the little boy and his companion in the best of humor. Stineli had fulfilled her promise about the story of Peterli's funny doings, and this had amused Silvio exceedingly. When the latter espied the violin, he cried out at once, "Now let us sing; let us sing the 'Lambkins' with Stineli."

Stineli had never heard her song since it was composed that day on the mountain, for now Rico played such beautiful airs that she had quite forgotten the old ones. But she was astonished to hear Silvio asking for the German song, for she had no idea of the hundred times the two boys had repeated it during the three years that were past. She was much pleased to hear the old song again, and, above all, to sing it with Rico; and so they began. Silvio sang with all his might,--without understanding a single word, to be sure, but the tune was quite correct. It was the girl's turn to laugh now; for Silvio's pronunciation was most wonderful, and she could not join in for laughter, and it was contagious; for the child could not resist the merry expression of her face, and joined her in laughing, and sang again still more queerly and louder; and all the while Rico played his accompaniment without stopping.

And thus Mrs. Menotti's ears were greeted with laughter and song as she drew near the house on her return, and she could not understand how they could be so light-hearted and merry on such a momentous occasion. She came hastily through the garden, and into the room, and sank upon the nearest seat; for the shock and the joy, and the anticipation of what was to follow, had overpowered her, and she needed to recover herself a little. The sight of her agitation silenced the singers, and they gazed at her in surprise. At last she recovered, and said,--

"Rico,"--and her voice was quite solemn,--"Rico, listen to me. Look about you. This house, this garden, that field,--all, all that you can see, and much that you cannot see, belongs to you: it is all yours. You are the owner; it is your inheritance from your father; your home is here; your name stands in the baptismal record; you are the son of Henrico Trevillo, and he was my husband's dearest friend."

Stineli had understood the whole story at the first word, and her face beamed with unspeakable happiness.

Rico sat as if turned to stone, and made no sound; but Silvio broke out into shouts of delight,--it was all a play to him.

"Oh! now the house belongs to Rico, where is he going to sleep?"

"He can sleep in any room he chooses, Silvio. He can sleep in them all if he wishes to. He can turn us all out-of-doors if he has a mind to, and stay all sole alone in this house."

"I am sure I should much prefer to go away with you, then," said Rico.

"Oh, you good Rico!" cried Mrs. Menotti. "If you will let us stay here, we shall be so glad to remain. I have thought it out as I came along towards home, and know how we can arrange it so that we shall be happy. I will take half of the house of you, and the same with the garden and all the land; so one half will be yours, and the other Silvio's."

"I shall give my half to Stineli," said the child.

"So shall I," said Rico.

"Oh, ho! now the whole thing belongs to her,--the garden, and the house, and all that is in them; and Rico and his fiddle, and I too. Now let us go on with our song."

But Rico did not take the same view of the affair as his little friend. He had thought over Mrs. Menotti's words, and now asked, anxiously,--

"I do not understand how Silvio's house can belong to me because our fathers were friends."

It now occurred to Mrs. Menotti for the first time that Rico did not know any thing about the circumstances; and she told him the whole story, with all the particulars, even more minutely than she had told it to Stineli; and when she had finished they all understood perfectly how it was, and were at liberty to rejoice without restraint; for since the house and all belonged partly to Rico, there was no reason why he should not take possession at once, and never leave them again; and their rejoicing was great.

In the midst of their merry-making Rico said, suddenly,--

"Since things have turned out this way, Mrs. Menotti, do not let any of the arrangements be disturbed in the house; but every thing go on as usual. I will simply come here to live, and you shall be our mother."

"O Rico! to think that it is yours, that it is you who are the **master**. How good God is to let it all turn out in this way,--that I can give it all to you, and yet stay here myself with a clear conscience. I will be a mother to you, Rico; and indeed you have long been as dear to me as if you were my own child. Now you must call me 'mother,' and so must Stineli; and we shall be the happiest household in all Peschiera."

"Well, now let us finish our song," cried little Silvio; for he was so excited and glad that he felt that singing was the only way to express his joy; and the others were not unwilling to join him, and they did finish their song; then Stineli said,--

"Now will you not sing one other song with me, Rico? You know which one I mean."

And they sang the grandmother's hymn piously, and in beautiful accord, especially the favorite verses at the end,--

"He never yet has done amiss;
And, perfect in His sight,
All that He does or orders is
Sure to be finished right.
"Now only let His 'will be done,'
Nor clamor constantly,
Peace to the heart on earth will come,
And joy eternally."

The next day Rico did not go to Riva. Mother Menotti advised him to go at once to the landlady, to explain to her the change in his circumstances, and to order another fiddler to be sent to Riva, while he at once entered upon his possessions. Well pleased with these suggestions, the youth hastened to carry them out.

The landlady heard his wonderful story with great interest, and at the end she called out to her husband and told it all over to him, and testified real pleasure at the good fortune that had befallen her young friend, and was sincere in what she said. She certainly was sorry to lose him; but she had suspected for some time that the hostess of the "Three Crowns" was making advances to Rico in the hope of enticing him away from her; and that would have been dreadful to the "Golden Sun." Now any danger of that misfortune was averted, and she was glad to hear that Rico was a house and land holder himself, for he was a great favorite with her. Her husband was particularly well pleased; for he had been a friend of Rico's father, and did not now understand why he had not earlier noticed that the lad was the exact image of the man.

So the farewells were all spoken in good feeling, and the landlady took his hand at parting, and asked for his patronage if ever there was occasion for her services in his house.

That very evening the news was known in all Peschiera, with all the true details, and a great many more; and everybody expressed pleasure, and said that Rico looked exactly as if he owned an estate, and would grace the position.

Mother Menotti did not know how she could do enough to make Rico comfortable in his own house. She arranged the big room for him--the one that had two windows overlooking the garden, and with a view over the lake--with beautiful marble statuettes adorning the walls; and on the table she placed a vase of flowers, and the whole room was most prettily furnished, so that Rico stood still on the threshold when, at Mrs. Menotti's request, Stineli led him up there. And when the kind, motherly woman took his hand and led him to the window, and he looked down in the shimmering lake, and over at the purple mountains in the distance, his heart filled to overflowing with thankfulness, and he could only murmur, softly,--

"Oh, how beautiful! And this is my home!" And now day after day the four happy friends lived their peaceful life in the comfortable room looking on the garden, where Silvio lay, and never perceived how the time was speeding away.

In the daytime Rico went about with his whistling servant lad through the fig-trees and over the fields planted with corn, for he wanted to learn the care of it all.

Now the servant naturally thought, "I know much more than my new master," and felt sensible of his superiority over Rico; but when, in the evening, beautiful and heart-stirring music came forth upon the evening breeze from the well-lighted room, where they all sat together, the boy leaned against the hedge and listened for long hours; for music was his greatest delight, and he said to himself, "My master knows more than I do, after all;" and he could not help feeling a great respect for Rico.

CHAPTER XXI.
SUNSHINE ON THE LAKE OF GARDA.

Two years have passed, every day bringing more enjoyment than the last.

To Stineli came the knowledge that it was time for her to return to her home, and she had many a hard battle with herself to keep up her courage and cheerfulness; for to go away, and probably never return, was the most dreadful prospect that ever presented itself to the young girl's imagination. Rico also knew what was before them, and sometimes he would only speak when it became absolutely necessary. And a strange, unnatural feeling took possession of mother Menotti, and she tried to discover the secret cause; for she had quite forgotten that Stineli was to go home again to be confirmed. When at last the cause of the trouble came out, she said, "Oh! you can put that off for another year;" and so things fell back into their old comfort again.

On the third year, however, a message came from Bergamo (some one came down there from the mountain) that Stineli was wanted at home, and must go. Now there was no help for it. Silvio might fight against it like one possessed: it did no good. Against fate it is useless to struggle.

Mother Menotti said, day after day, towards the end, "Only promise to come back, Stineli. You may tell your father I will do any thing he wishes, if he will only let you come back soon."

Rico said nothing at all. And Stineli went off; and day after day it seemed as if a big black cloud lay over the household, and as if the very sun outside had ceased to shine.

And so it went on from November to Easter, when everybody was rejoicing; but it was still sad in Rico's house. After the Easter festival was over, and every thing was beginning to be more beautiful than ever before in the garden, and flowers and sweet odors were spread all abroad, Rico sat by Silvio's bedside, and played every sad melody that he could remember, until the little fellow was in a most melancholy mood, when suddenly from the garden a merry voice called out,--

"Rico, Rico! have you no more cheerful welcome for me than this?"

Silvio screamed as if beside himself. Rico threw his violin on the bed, and ran out; and mother Menotti came in, half frightened.

On the threshold stood Rico with Stineli; and so in Silvio's room there was the long-lost sunshine back again, and they were as merry as ever again, and happy as they had never believed would be possible during their long separation. There they all sat at table by Silvio's bedside, and questioned and answered, and told all that had happened, and ever and again broke out into rejoicing over their reunion. Who would have thought, to see them there, that any thing could be wanting to the perfect happiness of these four people? But Rico knew another tale. In the midst of all the merriment, he became absent-minded, and fell into one of his old dreamy moods. It did not last as long as formerly, however. He must have reached a satisfactory conclusion pretty soon; for suddenly his reverie was over, and he said these words, with the utmost decision, "Stineli must be my wife this very moment, or else she will have to go away again directly; and that we could not endure."

This decision pleased Silvio mightily; and in a short time they were all of the same way of thinking, that the sooner the marriage took place the better.

On the very most beautiful May morning that ever shone over Peschiera, a long procession started from the church towards the "Golden Sun."

At the head, tall and well-proportioned, came Rico with his stately mien; and at his side walked Stineli, looking happy and pretty, her smooth braids crowned with the fresh bridal wreath. Next in the procession, in a well-upholstered little wagon, drawn by two merry Peschiera urchins, Silvio might be seen, beaming with satisfaction like a triumphant victor; and last of all followed mother Menotti, very much moved and affected, in a rustling wedding-dress; behind her the servant lad, with a nosegay that covered his whole shirt-front; and after them streamed all Peschiera, with the very noisiest kind of participation, for they all wanted to look at the handsome couple, and to do them honor. It was almost like a great family festival, in which they all joined to help the strayed and lost Peschiera boy to found his own home in his native town.

The joy of the landlady of the "Golden Sun," when she saw the procession coming towards her house, is quite indescribable. Whenever the question arose concerning any wedding, low or high, she always said, with emphasis,--

"That is nothing at all in comparison with Rico's wedding in the 'Golden

Sun.'"

The house in the garden never again lost its sunshine, and Stineli took good care "Our Father" was never forgotten again; and on every Sunday evening the grandmother's hymn was sung in the garden in full chorus.

HOW WISELI WAS PROVIDED FOR.

CHAPTER I.
COASTING.

O n one of the hills surrounding the city of Bern a little village is perched which shall be nameless in this story; but if you are curious, and go there in your travels, perhaps you may recognize it from the following description. On the very top of the hill stands one solitary house, with a beautiful garden about it. It is called "On the Height," and is the property of Colonel Ritter. The descent to the little square, where the church and parsonage stand, is sharp (in the parsonage the colonel's wife passed her happy days of childhood); and somewhat farther down is the schoolhouse, amid a little cluster of houses; while on the left, as you still descend, you see a lonely cottage with a pretty, well-kept garden, surrounded by currant-bushes, and adorned with mignonette and pinks, and a few roses amidst its chiccory and spinach. This is the last house on the road, which, from here on, makes one long stretch downward to the highway that goes far out into the country, parallel with the river Aar.

This long, unbroken descent forms, in winter, the most perfect coasting-ground imaginable; for once you are past the steep bit by the colonel's house, you may go on without interruption quite down to the road by the river; that is, always supposing that you make a fair start at the beginning.

This coast was an endless source of pleasure to the army of children who daily poured out of the door of the old schoolhouse when lesson hours were over, ran to the yard where they had piled their sleds on entering, took each his own from the heap, and scampered off in wild haste to begin their afternoon amusement. How the hours passed no one could imagine: down flew the sleds in a twinkling, and nobody felt the trouble of climbing up the hill, so full were all the little heads of the pleasure of going down again; and so the night, and the time for returning to their homes for supper, always took them by surprise.

This usually occasioned a stormy scene before they left the coasting-ground; for everybody wished to go down "once more," and then "just *once* more," and then "one single turn more,"--so that everybody hurried and jumped onto the sleds, and flew down and ran up again in a regular hurry-scurry.

A rule had been established to the end that no one should go down the coast while the others were still climbing up, but that all should go down one after the other in good order, to prevent confusion or accidents. Notwithstanding this good rule, there were often many lawless proceedings, especially towards the close of the day, when nobody wished to be the last, and when they all crowded onto the coast very closely together.

This was the state of affairs on a clear evening in January, when the snow fairly crackled under the children's feet as they mounted the hill, and the fields in every direction were frozen so firmly that you could have gone anywhere over them in a sleigh as if they were the highway. The children were all rosy and glowing with their exertions, for they were hurrying up the steep hill, pulling their sleds behind them, turning them about in a flash, jumping upon them, and off again head foremost, not to lose a second of the precious time until the moon shone brightly in the crisp sky, and the evening bells were ringing. All the boys were shouting, "Once more; just once more!" and the girls were as eager as they. At the top, however, where they all threw themselves upon their sleds, there was great excitement and uproar. Three boys each claimed to have reached the top first, and would not yield an inch to each other, but all must go down at once. And so they pushed this way and that, until a big boy called Cheppi was hustled quite against the bank of snow at the side of the coast, and found that his heavily ironed sled was fast in the snow. He was furious, for he saw that now all the other fellows would get off before he could extricate himself. He looked about, and presently espied a little slender girl standing near by in the snow. She was very pale, and held both arms wrapped in her apron to keep them warmer, for all that she trembled and shivered with cold from head to feet. She looked so feeble and miserable, that she seemed to Cheppi just the proper object upon whom to vent his rage.

"Can't you get out of a fellow's way, you stupid thing? What are you standing there for? You have not even a sled with you. Just wait a moment; I'll help you to get along!"

So saying, he thrust his boot into the snow, intending to kick it over the girl. She sprang back, however, quickly, so that she went quite up to her knees in the snow, and said timidly, "I was only looking on."

Cheppi was thrusting his boot into the snow again with the same intention towards the child, when he received such a tremendous box on the ear from behind, that it almost knocked him off his sled. "Just you wait a minute," he shouted, beside himself with anger, for his ear tingled as it had never tingled before; and doubling up his fists, he turned himself to see who was his hidden foe. A boy stood behind him, and looked on very quietly, holding his sled in position for another coast.

"Come on," he said calmly.

It was Otto Ritter, a class-mate of Cheppi, with whom he was always engaged in some little quarrel. Otto was a tall, slender boy, about eleven years old, and not nearly of the same strength as Cheppi; but the latter had learned more than once that with hands and feet Otto was much the more skilful of the two. He did not strike out, but held his fists doubled up, and cried out angrily, "Let me alone: I am not meddling with you."

"But I am with you," replied Otto, in a very warlike tone. "What business have you to chase Wiseli away like that, and then to kick snow at her, I should like to know? I have been looking at you, you coward! teasing a little girl who cannot defend herself."

With these words he turned his back contemptuously towards Cheppi, and called out to Wiseli, who was standing shivering all this time in the deep snow,--

"Come out of the snow, Wiseli. Oh, how you are shivering, child! Have you no sled really, and only been able to look on? Here, take mine, and go down once quickly. Do you know how?"

The pale, timid girl did not know what to make of this kindness. She had been looking on for some little time, watching the sleds as they flew down the hill, and thinking, "Oh, how I should like to go down to the very bottom just once!" when she saw two, and sometimes three, going down on the same sled. But now she might go down all alone by herself, and that, too, on the very handsomest sled on the coast,--the one with a lion's head, that went faster than any other, because it was light, and was bound with iron. She was so happy that she stood still, looking after Cheppi with a half feeling that he might strike her if she dared to enjoy such a piece of good fortune. But there he stood quite tranquilly, as if nothing whatever had happened; and by him stood Otto, with such a protecting air, that she took courage, and seated herself on the handsome sled; and when Otto called out, "Go on; go on, Wiseli!" she obeyed, and away she flew as if the wind were behind her. Very soon Otto heard the coasters all toiling up the hill again, and he called out, "Stay among the first, Wiseli, and go down again; after that we must go home." Wiseli was only too happy to do as she was bid, and enjoyed for a second time the long-wished-for pleasure. Then she brought the sled to its owner, thanking him shyly for his kindness, but more with her beaming eyes than with words; and off she scampered as fast as she could go. Otto felt decidedly happier. "Where is Pussy?" he called out, peering into the already scattering crowd. "Here she is!" replied a merry voice; and out of the knot of children appeared a red-cheeked, plump little girl, who slipped her hand into her big brother's protecting palm, and went with him towards their father's house as quickly as possible. It was very late, and they had over-passed the allotted time for coasting.

CHAPTER II.
AT HOME WHERE ALL ARE HAPPY.

When Otto and his sister came noisily in through the deep stone entrance of their father's house, the old servant Trine appeared in a doorway holding a light high above her head to see whence came all the uproar, and from whom. "So," at last she said, half scoldingly, half pleasantly; "your mother has been asking for you for a long time, but there was no trace of you, although it struck eight nobody knows how long ago." Old Trine had been maid-servant in the family when the children's mother came into the world, so she was an authority in the household, and felt that she was one of its members,--to tell the truth, the very head of the establishment; for surely she was the oldest in age and experience. The dear old woman was fairly foolish in her fondness for her master's children, and very proud of all their qualities and acquisitions. She would not let this be seen, however, but employed an indignant tone when speaking to them; for she thought it best for their education not to appear perfectly satisfied with their conduct.

"Off with your shoes, on with your slippers!" she called out at once, according to rule; but her order was immediately executed by the commander, for she knelt before Otto while she spoke, to take off his wet shoes. He had sunk down upon the nearest seat. His little sister stood perfectly still in the middle of the room without stirring, which was such an unusual circumstance, that Trine looked over her shoulder two or three times to see what it could mean. Now that Otto was equipped, it was Pussy's turn to sit down and be attended to; but she stood stock still, and did not stir. "Well, well! if we wait there until summer comes, our shoes will get dry of themselves," said Trine, still on her knees. "Hsh, hsh, Trine! I hear something. Who is in the big parlor?" said Pussy, lifting her forefinger up a little threateningly. "Everybody who has dry shoes: nobody else admitted. Now make up your mind to sit down," said Trine. But instead of sitting down, Pussy made a spring upward, and cried, "Now I hear it again; Uncle Max laughs just like that." "What!" cried Otto, and reached the parlor-door with one leap.

"Wait, wait!" Pussy called after him, and ran to the door at the same time; but she was caught and placed on the seat, although old Trine had hard work to get the shoes off the little kicking feet; but perseverance at last accomplished the business, and off ran Pussy out of one door and through the other into the big parlor, where truly sat Uncle Max in the arm-chair. Now there was a fine jubilee, and a hugging and kissing over and over. Uncle Max certainly made as much noise as the children, and it was a long time before they were quieted enough to speak a rational word to each other. A visit from this uncle was always a time of great delight for the children, and with good reason, for he was extravagantly fond of them. He was a great traveller, and only came to see them once in two years; but then he made up for his long absence by giving himself entirely to his little friends as if he were no older than they; and the queer and enchanting presents that he had stuffed into every pocket for his little niece and nephew would be hard to describe.

Uncle Max was a naturalist, and travelled to every corner of the world, bringing back something curious and interesting from each place.

At last supper was served, to the immense satisfaction of the whole party,--for the children always brought home new appetites from the coasting-ground, and were prepared, both old and young, to do full justice to the steaming dishes set before them.

"Well," said Colonel Ritter, glancing across the table at his little daughter, who was seated beside her mother, and already too busily engaged in satisfying her hunger to look up from her plate. "Well, well; it seems rather strange to think that Pussy has no hand to spare for her papa to-day. I have not had one single kiss, and now it is too late."

With a contrite air Pussy pushed back her plate, saying, "O papa, I forgot! I will give you"--

But her father said, quickly, "No, no; do not make a disturbance now, child. Give me your hand across the table; we will have the rest later. That will do now, Pussy."

"What was this child christened, Marie? I was certainly present at the ceremony, but I have utterly forgotten her name. Not Pussy, I am sure," said Uncle Max, laughing.

"You certainly were present, Max," replied his sister, "for you are the child's godfather. She was named Marie. At this time her father nicknamed her Pussy, and Otto has multiplied that in the most nonsensical manner."

"Oh, no, mamma; not nonsensical," cried Otto, quite seriously. "You see, uncle, it follows in very sensible order. When the little thing is gentle and good, then I call her 'Pussy.' That is not always the case, however, and 'Puss' does for some of her moods; but when she is angry, and looks like a regular cross-patch, then I call her 'Old Cat.'"

"Yes, yes, Otto," answered his sister; and when you are angry, you look like a--like a"--

"Like a man," said Otto; and as Pussy had no better comparison ready, she went on busily eating her pudding.

Uncle Max laughed heartily. "Pussy is right," he said. "She does far better in pursuing her present occupation than in answering back such slanders. But, children," he began again, after a pause, "it is more than a year since I was here, and you have not told me about any thing that has taken place during my absence."

The latest events were those that occurred first to the children; and they began to tell, generally both speaking together, the story of Cheppi's rude treatment of Wiseli on the coast, and of how cold the girl was, and how she stood shivering in the snow, and had no sled of her own, but got a chance to coast down twice after all.

"That is right, Otto," said his father. "You must honor your name. You must always be a true knight for the persecuted and unprotected. Who is this Wiseli?"

"You cannot know any thing about the girl nor her mother," said his wife. "But Uncle Max knows Wiseli's mother very well. You remember that thin weaver who was our neighbor, don't you, brother? He had an only daughter with big brown eyes, who often came to us at the parsonage, and sang so sweetly. Can't you remember her now?"

While Uncle Max was trying to recall the somewhat fading recollections of his youth, old Trine put her head into the room, saying,--

"The carpenter Andrew would like to speak to you, Mrs. Ritter, if it will not disturb you too much."

This apparently innocent message produced a wonderful effect upon the whole family. Mrs. Ritter put down the tablespoon, with which she was about to help her brother a second time to fruit, and said hastily, "If you will excuse me, gentlemen," and left the room. Otto sprang up so quickly that he knocked his chair over backwards, and then fell over it himself in his haste to get away. Pussy was about to follow the others; but her uncle, seeing the movement, put his arms about her, and held her fast. She struggled, however, and said, entreatingly,--

"Let me go, uncle; let me go. Really, I must go."

"Where do you want to go, Pussy?"

"To see the carpenter Andrew. Let me go quickly. Help, papa; help!"

"If you will tell me what you have to say to the carpenter, I will let you go."

"The sheep has only two legs left, and no tail at all; and the carpenter is the only person who can mend him. Now *do* let me go!" And now Pussy was off too.

The gentlemen looked at each other, and Max burst out into a merry laugh. "Who is this carpenter Andrew, pray, who seems to have the power of attracting your whole family to his feet?"

"You ought to be able to answer that question better than I," replied the colonel. "He must also be one of the friends of your youth. The fever of adoration you ought to understand also: it must be one of your family characteristics; and your sister has introduced it into her family. I can only tell you this much: this Andrew is the very corner-stone of my house. Every thing depends upon him, and we should all fall to pieces if his support were withdrawn from us. Andrew is the counsellor, comforter, safety, and aid in any trouble. If my wife thinks she wants any utensil for household use, even if she does not know how it should look, nor what use to put it too, Andrew the carpenter invents it, and makes it on the spot. If the kitchen is on fire, or the water gives out there, or in the laundry, Andrew the carpenter smothers the fire, and procures floods of water. If my son does some sad piece of mischief, Andrew the carpenter repairs the damage in a trice. If my daughter smashes all the crockery, Andrew the carpenter glues it together at once. So you see that this man is really the very pillar of my edifice; and if any thing should happen to him, we should straightway go to pieces."

Mrs. Ritter had returned to the room during this account of Andrew the carpenter's virtues, and her husband had heightened the description for her benefit. Uncle Max shouted with laughter.

"Yes, laugh away; laugh away!" said she. "For all that, I know very well what a treasure I possess in Andrew the carpenter."

"So do I, for that matter," said her husband, laughing merrily.

"I do, too," said Pussy, heartily, who was again on her seat at table.

"So do I," grumbled Otto, while he rubbed his shins, that ached from his recent fall over the chair.

"Well, now we are all of one mind about it, and the children can go quietly to bed," said their mother. These words did not tend to restore quiet, for the children became rebellious; but it was useless. Old Trine stood on the threshold, and was ready to carry out the family rules and regulations. Off marched the children, and presently their mother also disappeared again; for there were the evening prayers to be said, and she never failed to be at their bedside for that.

When, at last, every thing was in order in the house, Mrs. Ritter joined the gentlemen once more.

"At last!" said the colonel, with a sigh of relief, as if he had vanquished the enemy. "Now you see how it is, Max. My wife belongs first of all to the carpenter

Andrew, then to the children, and only to her husband when there is nothing else for her to do."

"And now you see, Max," said his sister, laughing, "that, although my husband speaks scornfully of Andrew the carpenter, he does assign him a very high rank after all. Now acknowledge that, won't you? He has just given me a message for you. He has brought his yearly savings with him to-day, and begs for your assistance."

"That is true," said the colonel. "A more orderly, industrious, reliable man I do not know. I would trust my wife, my children, my goods and chattels to him rather than to any one else. He is the most honorable, trustworthy man in this parish, or in any other, I do believe."

"Now you see, Max," said his sister, laughing, "I could not say more than that." Her brother joined with her in her amusement at the zest which the colonel showed. Then he said,--

"You have all been so full of the praises of your marvel, that I have become curious, at last, to know where he comes from, and how he looks. Have I never seen him when I have visited you?"

"Oh, yes! you used to know him perfectly well," replied his sister. "You must remember Andrew, with whom we went to school. Don't you recall the two brothers who were always in the same classes with you? The elder was even then a perfect good-for-nothing,--he was not stupid, but would not study, and did not get on, and was put down into one of the lower classes with his brother and you. You must remember him,--his name was Jorg, and he had stiff, black hair. He always pelted us with something whenever he got a chance,--with green apples or pears, and in winter with snow-balls,--and always called us 'aristocrats.'"

"Oh, that fellow!" cried Max. "Yes; now I do remember all about him. Certainly he always called us 'aristocrats.' I wonder how he got hold of that word. He was a disagreeable fellow: I remember that well. I caught him once thrashing a little fellow most cruelly. I helped the little one, and he shouted after me at least twelve times in succession, 'Aristocrat, aristocrat!' And now it comes back to me about the other one, the lean Andrew, his brother. He was your Andrew, was he not, Marie?--the Andrew with the violets? Oh, now I comprehend this great friendship," said Max, laughing again.

"What is this about the violets? I want to know all about that," said the colonel.

"Oh! I can see the whole thing just as it happened as plainly as if it were only yesterday," said Max, quite animated over his recollections. "I must tell you all about it, Otto. You have probably heard from your wife that we had here, in the happy time of our childhood, an old schoolmaster, whose creed was that all faults could be whipped out of, and all virtues be whipped into, the children under his care. So he felt himself constrained to whip a great deal either for one thing or the other, and very often for both at once. Andrew's turn came one day, and the master applied his well-meant rule so heartily that poor, thin Andrew screamed with pain. At this moment my little sister, who had only entered the school a short time before, and did not understand the rules very well, stood up from her seat and hastened to the door. The teacher held his hand for a moment, and shouted after her, 'Where are you running to?' Marie turned about. The tears were running down her cheeks, and she said, very decidedly, 'I am going home to tell my father.' 'Wait, I will teach you!' cried the master, in the greatest surprise, and sprung after the girl. He did not strike her, however, but took her roughly by the arm, and set her down very hard upon the bench; then he said again, 'Wait, I will teach you!'

"It was the end of that, however. He did not touch Andrew again, and every thing passed off quietly that day. But the tears that Marie had shed for Andrew, and her protest against the whippings, were not forgotten. From that day forward a big bunch of violets was always placed on Marie's desk, and the whole room was perfumed with them; and later a still better scent filled the air, for there were every day great bunches of dark red strawberries, such as nobody else knew how to find. And so it went on for the whole year; but how the friendship reached the height at which it now stands, that I will leave to my sister to relate, for I do not know myself."

The colonel was much pleased with this story of the tears and the violets, and begged his wife to tell more about it. She said, "According to you, Max, violets and strawberries grow all the year round; but, in truth, it is not exactly the fact. But it is true that the good Andrew was never tired of bringing in any thing that he thought would give me pleasure all through the time we were in the school together. He left long before I did, and went to learn his trade of a joiner in the city. He came home very often, however, so that I never really lost sight of him; and when my husband bought this piece of land and we were married, it happened, also, that Andrew bought property, and wished to be settled. He had lost his parents, and was quite by himself, and a first-rate workman. He wanted the little house with the neat, pretty garden down there half-way to the church; but was not able to purchase it, because the owner wished for full payment at once, and Andrew could only pay in instalments, as he earned the money.

"But we knew all about him and his work. My husband purchased the place for him, and he has never had the least reason to regret it."

"No, indeed I have not," added the colonel. "Andrew has long ago paid for his house, and now he always brings me the yearly amount of his labor; and a very pretty sum it is, too. I invest it well for him, and have a sincere satisfaction in the welfare of the sturdy fellow. He is already a very well-to-do man, and adds to his property every year, and can make his little house into a big one if he have a mind to do so, the good Andrew. It is too bad that he is such a hermit, and cannot, therefore, properly enjoy his home and his possessions."

"Has he, then, neither wife nor family?" asked Max. "And what has become of his disagreeable brother Jorg?"

"No; he has really nobody," replied his sister. "He lives entirely alone, and really like a hermit. He has had a long and very sad history that I have been witness to, and which has taken away all the desire he once might have felt to look for a wife. His brother Jorg wandered about here in a disreputable way for several years, never working, but in the hope of getting something, by his infamous behavior, out of his family, who were respectable people, quite unlike himself. But, at last, he saw that there was no chance of this, and even the kind Andrew refused to pay any more of his debts, or to help him out of any more scrapes, so he disappeared, nobody knows where; but everybody rejoiced that he was out of the way."

"What was the sad story of which you spoke, Marie?" asked her brother. "I want to hear that, too."

"So do I," said the colonel; and lighted another cigar, in order to enjoy the tale more thoroughly.

"But, my dear husband," objected his wife, "I have at least told you this story ten times over."

"Really," said the colonel, quietly, "it seems that it pleases me then, if I ask for it again."

"Oh, do begin!" said her brother.

"You cannot have forgotten the child, Max," began his sister, "of whom I was speaking yesterday, who lived quite near to us. She belonged to the pale, thin weaver, whose shuttle we could always hear moving back and forth when we stood in our garden. The child always looked clean and neat, and had great lively, sparkling eyes, and beautiful brown hair. Her name was Aloise."

"I never knew anybody by the name of Aloise in my life," interrupted Max at this point.

"Oh! to be sure not," said his sister. "We never called her so, you especially. 'Wisi' we called her, to the horror of our dear departed mother. Don't you remember, now, how often you said yourself that we must get Wisi to sing with us when mamma played songs for us on the piano, and we could not make it go at all without Wisi's help?"

At last Max seemed to remember about it, and laughed at the recollection. "Oh, yes! I remember Wisi," he cried. "Yes, certainly that was Wisi. I can see her now, before my eyes, with her bright face, as she stood by the piano and sang so cheerily. I was very fond of her. I was very fond of her,--of Wisi. She was very pretty, too. I remember, too, what a shock it always seemed to mamma when I said, 'Wisi.' I really never knew her proper name."

"Oh, yes, you did," replied his sister; "because mamma always said it was perfectly barbarous to change the pretty name of Aloise into 'Wisi.'"

"I certainly never heard it each time," said Max. "But pray what has become of this Wisi?"

"You remember she was in my class at school, and we kept along together; and I often think of how Andrew always befriended and stood up for the girl through thick and thin, and that she knew well how to turn his friendship to good account.

"When she came with her slate full of examples, like the rest of us, her figures were not often correct; but she put the slate, with a merry laugh, on her desk, and lo! soon the sums were all rightly set down, for Andrew had put them in order. It often happened that she smashed a pane in the schoolroom window, or shook down the schoolmaster's plums in the garden; and yet Andrew was always the one who took the blame of these misdeeds,--not that anybody accused him, but he himself used to say, half aloud, that he believed it was his fault that the glass was broken, or the plums shaken down, and so he got the punishment. We children all knew well enough who was to blame; but we let it go, we were so used to it, and were so fond of the merry Wisi, that we all were pleased when she escaped punishment.

"Wisi had always pocketfuls of apples, pears, and nuts, that all came from Andrew; for every thing that he had, or could procure, he used to stuff into Wisi's satchel. I used often to wonder how it happened that the quiet Andrew liked the very most unruly and gayest girl in the school, and I also wondered whether she returned his affection. She was always very friendly with him, but she was the same with others; and as I once asked our mother how it could be, she shook her head a little, and said, 'I am afraid,--I am afraid that the nice little Aloise is a trifle heedless, and may have to suffer for it.' These words gave me much food for thought, and recurred to me again and again.

"We went together to the Bible-class; and every Sunday evening Wisi used to come regularly to our house, and we sang hymns together to the piano. She particularly enjoyed this. She knew all the lovely songs by heart, and sang them clearly and well; and mamma and I were very much pleased to know that Wisi liked to sing, and went gladly to the Bible-class, and seemed to take the religious teaching very much to heart. She had grown into a fine large girl now, with bright eyes; and, although she did not look very strong, like the peasant girls in the villages, still she had a fine color, and was far prettier than any of them.

"At this time Andrew was learning his trade in the town, but invariably came home on Sundays. He always came up to the parsonage to call, and was inclined to talk to me about our former schooldays; and gradually we worked round to Wisi, and talked about her most of the time. Andrew spoke most eloquently and feelingly on this subject; and, although everybody else had adopted the name 'Wisi' for Aloise, he never called her so, but said 'Wiseli' so softly and prettily, that it was very sweet to hear.

"But one Sunday (we were not quite eighteen years old, Wisi and I,--mamma was with us that evening) Wisi came in looking very rosy, and said that she had come to tell us that she was betrothed to a young workman who had come lately to live in the village, and that they would soon be married, as he had a good position,

and it was arranged that they could be married in about twelve days. I was so surprised, and so sorry, that I could not say a word. Neither did my mother speak for a
long time, but looked very much troubled.

"After a time she talked very seriously with Wisi,--told her that it was foolish
in her to have taken up so quickly with a workman of whom she really could know
very little, and especially when there was another who had sought her for long
years, and plainly shown her how much he loved her; and, at last, she asked her if it
could not be broken off, this engagement,--or, at least, put off for a while, Wisi was
still so young, and ought to remain with her father. Then Wisi began to cry, and
said that it was all arranged; that she had given her promise, and that her father was
pleased. So my mother said no more about it; but poor Wisi cried bitterly, until my
mother took her by the hand, and led her to the piano, and said kindly, 'Dry your
tears: we will sing together.' And she played the accompaniment, and we sang,--

"'To God you must confide
Your sorrow and your pain;
He will true care provide,
And show you heaven again.
"'For clouds and air and wind
He points the path and way;
Your road He'll also find,
Nor let your footsteps stray.'

"After this, Wisi left us apparently comforted, and my mother spoke kindly
to her at parting; but I felt very sadly about the whole affair. I had a conviction
that poor Wisi had passed her happiest days, and would never be light-hearted
again; and I could not express my sorrow for Andrew. What would he say? He
said nothing,--not one word,--but went about for several years like a shadow, and
became more silent than ever, and had no longer the quietly happy expression that
formerly distinguished him."

"Poor fellow!" cried Max. "And did he never marry?"

"Oh, no, Max!" replied his sister, rather reproachfully. "How could he do so?
How can you ask such a question? He is faithfulness personified."

"How could I know that, dearest sister?" said Max soothingly. "I could not be expected to know that your gifted and inestimable friend possessed also the quality of steadfastness. But tell me some more about Wisi. I hope, truly, that the merry creature was not unfortunate. It would grieve me sadly to think that."

"I see plainly, brother, that all your sympathies are secretly with Wisi; and that you are not sorry for the faithful Andrew, whose heart was nearly broken when he found that he had lost her."

"Yes, yes," said Max. "I have the greatest sympathy for the good fellow. But do tell me how it was with Wisi: did she cry her pretty eyes out?"

"Almost, I believe," replied Marie. "I did not see her very often, and she had a great deal of work to do. I believe that her husband was not a bad fellow; but there was something very rough about him, and he was rude and unkind even to his own little children. Wisi had a hard time of it. She had a good many pretty children; but they were very delicate, and she lost them one after the other. Five she buried, and has only now one tender little girl,--a little Wiseli,--who is not much larger than our Pussy, though she is several years older. Naturally Wisi's health has been sadly tried with all this, and it is plainly visible now that it has almost reached the end with her. She is rapidly wasting away in consumption. I fear that there is no hope for her."

"Oh!" cried Max, "is this possible? Is it really so bad as that? Can nothing be done, Marie? Let us look after her, and try if we cannot mend matters somewhat."

"Oh, no! there is no chance for her," said his sister, sadly. "From the very beginning Wisi was too delicate for all the work and care that came upon her."

"And what became of her husband?"

"Oh! I quite forgot the sad trouble that poor Wisi had to endure with him also.

"About a year ago, he broke an arm and a leg in the workshop, and was brought home half dead. He was very ill, and could not work, and certainly was not a patient sufferer. Wisi had the care of him in his sickness, in addition to every thing else, and he died about six months after the accident. Wisi has lived alone with her child since that time."

"Then there will soon be nothing left but a little Wiseli, and what will become of her? But, no; it will not turn out so sadly, I am sure. Wisi will get well, and every thing be right again, as it should have been in the beginning."

"No, not so, Max; it is too late for that," replied his sister, decidedly. "Poor Wisi had to suffer sadly for her folly. But it is too late indeed!" she said, rising, almost frightened to see that it was after midnight, and that the colonel, who had been silent for some time past, was now sleeping in his arm-chair.

Max was not in the least sleepy, however. All this story of poor Wisi had awakened in him such lively recollections of his childhood, that he wanted to talk about many other events and people; but his sister was not to be persuaded. She took her bed-candle, and insisted upon going to bed.

There was nothing to be done but to awaken his brother-in-law, which he did with such a tremendous thump on the back, that the colonel sprang up with the feeling that he had been struck by an enemy's bomb-shell. But Max tapped him kindly on the shoulder, saying, "It is only a gentle warning from your wife that we must all beat a retreat." This was accomplished, and soon the house on the height stood quietly in the moonlight; and half way down the hill stood another house, where it would soon be silent, too, though a still feeble light glimmered there, casting a pale shadow through the little window out into the brilliant moonlit night.

CHAPTER III.
ALSO AT HOME.

At the same time that the colonel's children were going home, the little Wiseli ran along down the hill as fast as she could scamper, for she knew she had remained away longer than her mother liked that she should, and she very rarely did any thing of the kind. This evening had been one of such unusual pleasure for her that she had quite forgotten to go home at the usual time, and therefore ran all the faster, and so almost fell against a man, in her haste, who came out of the door of their cottage as she was rushing in. He stepped quietly to one side, and Wiseli hastened into the room, and went to her mother's side. To her great surprise, she found no light in the room,--her mother was sitting in the twilight, on a low chair by the window. "Mother," said the child, "are you angry because I was away such a long time?" and she put her arms around her mother's neck as she spoke. "No, no, Wiseli," said her mother, kindly; "but I am glad that you have come at last." The girl began at once to tell her mother about the delightful coast she had had on Otto's pretty sled,--how she had gone twice down the hill, and how pleasant it was. When she had finished her little story, she noticed, for the first time, how very quiet her mother was,-- much more so than usual,--and she asked anxiously, "Why have you not lighted the lamp, mother?"

"I feel so weary this evening, Wiseli," replied her mother, "that I could not get up to light it. Go get it now, my child, and bring me a little water to drink at the same time, I am so very thirsty." Wiseli hastened to the kitchen, and soon returned with the light in one hand, and in the other a bottle filled with red syrup, that looked so temptingly clear and good, that the thirsty invalid called out eagerly, "What is that you are bringing me? It looks so good!"

"I do not know," said the child; "it was standing on the kitchen-table. See how it sparkles!" Her mother took the bottle, and smelled at it. "Oh!" she said, smelling again, "it is like fresh, wild strawberries. Give me some water, quickly, Wiseli; I must drink." The child poured some of the red syrup into a glass, and filled it with water, which her mother swallowed eagerly, as one parched with thirst. "You do not know how refreshing it is, child," as she handed back the empty glass. "Put it away, Wiseli, but not far. It seems to me as if I could drink it all the time, I am so thirsty. Who brought me this refreshment, Wiseli: do you know? It must be from Trine: she brought it from the colonel's."

"Did Trine come in here, mother?" asked the child.

"No; I have not seen her at all," said her mother.

"Then it is not Trine, I am sure," said Wiseli, decidedly. "She always comes into the room when she brings anything for you. But Andrew the carpenter came today: did not he bring this with him?"

"What, Wiseli," said her mother, very eagerly, "what are you saying? Andrew the carpenter never came to see me: what made you think of that?"

"He was here, certainly; certainly he was here within this house. He went out of the door so quickly that I almost ran into him. Did you not hear him at all?"

Her mother was quiet for a long time without speaking; then she said, "I did hear the kitchen door softly opened. At first I thought it might be you, and--it is true, I did not hear you enter until later. Are you sure, Wiseli, that Andrew the carpenter was the person who went out from our door?"

Wiseli was sure of her affair, and told her mother exactly how the coat and how the cap looked that Andrew wore, and how frightened he was when she almost ran into him; so that, at last, she convinced the good woman, who said softly, as if to herself, "Yes, it must be Andrew; he knows what I like best."

"Now I remember something else, mother," cried Wiseli, quite excitedly. "Now I know for sure who once placed a big pot of honey in the kitchen,--you remember how much you liked that,--and then the apple-cakes a day or two ago,--do not you remember? You wished to send your thanks by Trine when she brought you something from the colonel's kitchen, and she said that she knew nothing at all about them. Now I am sure that Andrew the carpenter brought them, and secretly placed them in the kitchen for you."

"Now I believe so, also," said her mother, and softly wiped her eyes.

"There is nothing sad about it, mother," said Wiseli, rather shocked to see how often her mother kept wiping her eyes.

"You must thank him for me, Wiseli: I cannot. Tell him that I send him my thanks for all the goodness he has shown me,--he has always been kind to me. Come, sit down here by me a little," said she, softly. "Give me some more of the syrup, and then come and repeat the verse that I taught you the other day."

Wiseli brought more water, and mixed it with the syrup again, and her mother drank of it eagerly; then she laid her head wearily upon the low window-sill, and beckoned her little daughter to come to her side. It seemed to the child that her mother could not be comfortable, and she fetched a pillow from the bed, and placed it carefully under her mother's head. Then she sat down close to her side on a footstool, and held her mother's hand in her own, and complied with her request to repeat the verses, thus,--

"'To God you must confide
Your sorrow and your pain;
He will true care provide,
And show you heaven again.
"'For clouds and air and wind
He points the path and way;

Your road He'll also find,
Nor let your footsteps stray.'"

As Wiseli finished, she observed that her mother was almost asleep; but she heard her say, softly, "Think of this, my Wiseli; and when you do not know which way to turn, and every thing seems difficult and perplexing, then say to yourself these words,--

"'Your road He'll also find,   Nor let your footsteps stray.'"

Now the weary head sank down to rest, and little Wiseli would not awaken her mother by a movement, but nestled up to her quietly, and slept also. And the feeble light of the little lamp burned dimly in the quiet room,--more and more feebly it burned, until it slowly flickered and went out, and the cottage stood a dark object in the bright moonlight.

The next morning the neighbor from the nearest house stopped, as usual, on her way to the fountain, to look through the window of the cottage to see if all was well within. She saw that the sick woman was sleeping on the pillow, with her head against the window-sill, and that Wiseli stood weeping by her side. This seemed so strange, that she put her head a little way into the room, and asked, "What is the matter, Wiseli? Is your mother worse?" The child sobbed dreadfully, and could scarcely say, "I do not know what ails my mother."

The poor child had a strong suspicion of what it all meant, but she could not realize that her mother was lost to her. For she was still there, but asleep,--asleep for all the rest of her daughter's life on earth,--and could not hear how sadly the child called to her. The neighbor stepped to the window and looked at the sleeping head upon the pillow; then she started back in alarm. "Run quickly, Wiseli; run and fetch your cousin Gotti. He must come at once. You have no other relation, and somebody must look after things here. Run as fast as you can: I will wait here until you come back."

The child ran, but not fast, her heart was so heavy within her, and her limbs trembled; and at last she had to stop and give way to her tears, for she became more and more sure, with every step, that her mother would never waken more. But she went on again soon, although she could not stop her tears, for her sorrow increased as she went. In the beech grove, full a quarter of an hour's walk from the church, stood the house of her cousin Gotti; and presently Wiseli entered the door, still crying bitterly. Her cousin's wife stood in the kitchen, and asked harshly, "What is the matter with you?" Wiseli replied, between her sobs, that the neighbor had sent her to ask her cousin Gotti to come quickly to her mother. Probably the woman suspected, from the child's look, that her mother was more ill, for she spoke a little less roughly than usual. "I will tell him. You can go home: he is not here now." So Wiseli turned about, and reached home more quickly than she came, for she was returning to her mother. The neighbor stood by the doorstep,--she could not wait inside the room: it was not pleasant to her. But the child stepped in, and went to her place by her mother's side that she had kept all through the night. There she sat weeping, and only said, now and then, softly, "Mother." But no answering word came to her. At last Wiseli said, bending over her, "Mother, you can hear me, although you are in heaven now, and I cannot hear your answer." And the child sat holding her mother's hand tightly until long after noontime. About that time her cousin Gotti entered the room, looked about him a little, and then called for the neighbor. "You must arrange things here a little,--you know what I mean," he said,--"so that things will be ready for the removal. Then carry the keys away with you, so that nothing will be taken." He then turned to Wiseli and said, "Where are your clothes, little one? Get them together and tie them up in a bundle, and we will go away."

"Where shall we go?" asked the child.

"We will go home to the beech grove. You can stay there with us, for you have nobody else in the world now but your cousin Gotti."

At these words, Wiseli felt herself stiff with fear. Go to the beech grove, and live with them there,--was that her fate? She had always had the greatest fear of the wife of her cousin Gotti, and always stood a long time before the door, when she was sent there with a message, before she could summon courage to enter. The eldest son, Cheppi,--that rough fellow,--lived there, and Hannes and Rudi; and they threw stones at all the children. Was that to be her home?

Fear caused the child to turn pale and immovable.

"You must not be frightened, my child," said her cousin Gotti, in a kindly tone. "There are more people in our house than there are here, but it is all the more lively for that."

Wiseli put her things silently together in a shawl, and tied the two corners together crosswise; then she tied her scarf about her head, and stood ready.

"So," said her cousin, "now we will go," and turned towards the door; but Wiseli sobbed out suddenly,--

"Then I must leave my mother all alone."

With these words she ran to her mother, and clasped her in her arms again.

Her cousin Gotti stood rather disconcerted, and looked on. He did not know how to explain how things were with her mother, if she did not understand without words; for he was not strong in the matter of expressing himself: he had never given himself the trouble to try. At last, he said,--

"Now come, come along. A little child like you must be obedient. Come; and, after this, no crying. That does not mend matters one bit."

The child swallowed her sobs, and followed the cousin Gotti silently through the door. Once only she glanced backward, and said softly, "God will watch over you, mother;" and then went forth with her bundle on her arm, and left the little house which had been home to her. Just as she and her cousin Gotti went together across the field, Trine came towards them down the road, with a covered basket on her arm. The neighbor stood in the doorway, and looked after the departing couple. Trine went towards her, saying,--

"To-day I am bringing the sick woman something good. A little late, to be sure. We have Uncle Max on a visit to us: that always makes me late."

"And even if you had come early in the morning, you would have come too late to-day. She died last night."

"That cannot be!" cried Trine, startled. "Oh, goodness me! what will my lady say?"

With these words she turned sharp about, and ran home as fast as possible. The neighbor went back into the quiet room, and performed the last kind offices for Wiseli's mother.

CHAPTER IV.
AT COUSIN GOTTI's.

When Wiseli made her entry into her cousin Gotti's house at Beech Grove, the three boys came running out of the barn, and, behind Wiseli, into the room, where they placed themselves in front of her in a row, and stared at the timid little thing with all their eyes. Her cousin's wife came out of the kitchen, and stared also at the little thing, as if she had never seen her before.

Her cousin Gotti seated himself behind the table, and said,--

"I think she can eat something: she has not had much to-day. Come here," he said, turning to Wiseli, who stood all this time in the same place, with her bundle under her arm. She obeyed. Now her cousin's wife put new wine and cheese on the table, also a huge loaf of black bread. Cousin Gotti cut a big slice, put a lump of cheese upon it, and pushed it towards the child. "There, eat, little one," he said. "You must be hungry, I'm sure."

"No, I thank you," said Wiseli, softly. She could not have swallowed even a crumb. She felt as if she were crushed under her load of sorrow and anxiety, and could scarcely even breathe.

The boys stood there all the time, and stared at her.

"Don't be frightened," said cousin Gotti, encouragingly. "Do eat something." But the child sat motionless, and did not touch her bread. Her cousin's wife came again; and, putting her hands on her hips, stood looking her over from head to foot.

"If you don't want it," she said, "you can leave it;" and turned on her heel, and went again into the kitchen.

When cousin Gotti had refreshed himself sufficiently he arose, and said, "Put it in your pocket. By and by you will feel like eating, only do not feel frightened;" and he went into the kitchen. Wiseli tried to do as he told her, to put the bread and cheese into her pocket; but they were too large, and she put them back upon the table again.

"I will help you," said Cheppi, snatching the pieces from the table; and was about to stuff them into his open mouth, but they flew up into the air instead, for Hannes had knocked Cheppi's hand up with a smart blow, and so the plunder was scattered, and Rudi darted upon it, and carried part of it away. With this the two oldest boys fell upon him, and they kicked and cuffed, and screamed and shouted, until Wiseli was terribly frightened. Presently their father opened the kitchen-door, and called out, "What does this all mean?" Then the boys all answered at once, from the floor; and one said, "Wiseli did not want it;" and another, "Wiseli had not any;" and "As long as Wiseli did not want any"--

Their father called out, loudly, "If you do not stop that, I will come in with the thong, and whip you." And he slammed the door again.

"It" did not "stop," however; but, as soon as the door was shut again, it began worse than ever, for Hannes found that the best way to treat the enemy was to grasp him by the hair; and so they all seized each other by the hair, and stood in a ring, uttering terrible noises. In the kitchen their mother sat on a stool, and peeled potatoes. When her husband closed the door again, she asked,--

"What is your idea about that child? Why did you bring her home with you at once?"

"I thought she would have to stay with somebody. I am her cousin Gotti, and she has no other relatives. You can make her useful. She can do what you are doing now. Then you will be able to do other things. You are always saying that the boys give you so much work,--more than is right."

"Yes, as regards them, a great help she will be! You can hear now what a racket there is in there, and she is only a quarter of an hour in the house."

"I have heard that sort of thing a good many times before the little one came. I do not think that she has much to do with it," said the cousin Gotti quietly.

"Oh, you did not hear them!" said his wife sharply; "how they kept calling out something about Wiseli?"

"Well, they may call out, if they want to," said their father. "You will soon have the little one in hand. I think she is not a troublesome child,--I noticed that in the beginning,--and is much more obedient than those boys of yours."

This was too much for his wife.

"I do not see what is the use of finding fault with the boys," she said; and she peeled the potatoes faster and faster. "And I *should* like to know where the girl is to sleep."

Her husband pushed his cap back and forth several times upon his head, and said, soothingly,--

"One can't think of every thing at once. She must have had a bed to sleep in; and she can, at least, have that. Tomorrow I will go to the pastor. To-night she can sleep on the bench by the stove. It is always warm there; and I can put a partition in the little passage that goes into our room later, and set her bed in there."

"I never heard of bringing home a child and getting a bed for it a week afterwards," said the woman crossly; "and I should like to know who will pay for it if we must build something more for her into the bargain."

"When the parish assigns the child to us, they will allow us something for her maintenance. I shall take her cheaper than any one else would do, and she will be more comfortable here too."

With this the cousin went out into the shed, and called out for Cheppi to come with him. It was hard for the cousin's wife to make herself heard in the room when she wished to give this message. They were all fighting away, and shouting angrily and loudly.

"I am surprised that you sit there looking on, and do not try to quiet them in the least," said their mother to Wiseli, who sat cowering against the wall, and did not dare even to move. Cheppi, however, was dispatched to the barn, and the two others ran after him.

"Do you know how to knit?" the cousin's wife asked Wiseli, who replied, timidly, "Yes, I can knit stockings."

"Well, then, take this," she said; and took from the cupboard a big brown stocking, with yarn almost as stout as Wiseli's little fingers. "Go on with the foot," she said, "and take care to make it big enough: it is for your cousin Gotti." Then she went back into the kitchen, and the little girl took her seat on the bench by the stove, with the long stocking coiled up in her lap,--for it was so heavy that she could scarcely knit if it hung down: it pulled the needles out of her hand. She had scarcely begun to work, however, before her cousin's wife came in again.

"I think you had better come out into the kitchen with me," she said. "Then you can see how I do things, and be able to help me a little by and by." Wiseli obeyed, and watched her cousin's wife at her work as well as she was able; but the tears kept coming into her eyes so that she could scarcely see, for she thought all the time of how she used to go about in the kitchen with her mother, who chattered so pleasantly with her, and how they would stop to kiss each other now and then. She knew very well that she ought not to give way to her tears, and tried to swallow her sobs, until she felt almost strangling.

"See here, look here," said the cousin's wife, every now and then; "then you will know how to do it by and by." And she went about, here and there, in the kitchen, letting Wiseli stand, and said nothing else to her. This went on for some time, when there was a terrible stamping in the entry, and the woman said, "Open the door as quick as you can: they are coming." The noise was made by the cousin and his sons, who were knocking the snow off their shoes before entering. Wiseli opened the door into the inner room as quickly as possible; and the cousin's wife lifted an enormous pan off the fire, and ran with it into the room, where she shook a great heap of potatoes out over the slate-topped table. Then she brought out a big jug of sour milk, and said, "Put the things that are in the table-drawer on the table, and then they can all sit down at once."

Wiseli pulled out the drawer as quickly as possible. There lay five spoons and five knives. She put these upon the table, and the supper was ready. The father and his sons came in, and sat down at once on the seats along the wall behind the table. At the other end stood a chair. Cousin Gotti made a motion towards the chair and said, "She can sit there, I think; or do you say no?"

"Oh, certainly!" said his wife, whose seat was nearest the kitchen-door. She did not remain seated a moment; but ran out into the kitchen and came back, took a spoonful of milk, and was off again.

Nobody knew why she ran about in this way, for there was nothing cooking in the kitchen, and nothing to bring out, but she always did so; and when, sometimes, her husband would say, "Do sit still, and eat something," then she seemed more hurried than ever, and said she had no time to sit still, there were so many things to be looked after.

When she had made two visits to the kitchen and returned, and began to peel a potato in great haste, she noticed, for the first time, that Wiseli sat idly by her side, her hands on her lap. "Why don't you eat something?" she said, angrily. "She has no spoon," said Rudi, who was seated on the other side, and had long been wondering why anybody should sit at table and not eat as long as there was any thing left. "Oh, yes, of course," said his mother. "Who would ever have thought that we should need six spoons? We have always found five enough; and we must have another knife too. Why can't you speak? You know well enough that to eat you want a spoon." These last words were addressed to Wiseli.

The child glanced timidly at the woman and said, "It is no matter: I do not need any. I am not hungry."

"Why not?" asked the woman. "Are you used to a different kind of food? I don't mean to change, if you are."

"I think it would be better to let the child alone for a while; we must not frighten her," said her cousin Gotti, soothingly. "She will feel better soon."

So Wiseli was unmolested, and the others were busily employed for a while. She sat there motionless until her cousin rose, took his fur cap from the nail, and began to look for the stable lantern; for "Spot" was sick, and must be looked after again that night. The table was quickly cleared. The empty potato-skins were brushed off into the empty milk-jug, the slate-top wiped off; and when the woman was done with this, she said, turning to Wiseli, "You have seen what I did; now you can do it the next time." Now Cheppi took his seat firmly behind the table again. He had his slate-pencil and arithmetic book, and prepared himself to do his examples. First, however, he stared for a while at Wiseli, who had again taken up her brown stocking, but did not make any progress; for she could not see a thing in the dark corner where she was seated, and she did not dare to draw nearer to the table where the dim lamp was placed. "You must have something to do," cried Cheppi, in an irritated tone. "You are not the smartest scholar in the school." The girl did not know what to answer. She had not been to school that day, and did not know what lessons were given out; and, besides, was quite out of her usual habits and life generally. "If I must do my examples, so must you, or I won't do them at all," cried Cheppi again. Wiseli kept as still as a mouse. "Well, then, it is all right," said the boy noisily. "I won't do another stroke of work." And he threw away his pencil.

"Then I won't do any thing, either," cried Hannes, and stuffed his multiplication-table into his satchel again; for learning his lessons was the hardest thing in the world for him.

"I will tell the master whose fault it is," began Cheppi again. "You can see, then, what you will get."

Probably Cheppi would have gone on in this unpleasant style for a long time, if his father had not soon returned from the barn. He brought in two big, empty grain-bags on his shoulders, and came up to the table with them.

"Make room," he said to Cheppi, who sat with his elbows on the table, supporting his head on his hands. Then he spread out his two bags, folded them together again, and then again. At last he went towards the bench behind the stove, and put them down on it. "There," he said, with an air of satisfaction, "that is good. Where is your bundle, little one?" Wiseli fetched it from her corner,--where it had lain ever since she arrived,--and looked with surprise at her cousin Gotti as he placed the bundle at the upper end of the folded bags, and pressed it down, so that it was not perfectly round.

"There, now you may go to sleep," he said, turning round to Wiseli. "You cannot be cold, for the stove is hot; and you can put your head on your bundle, and you will be as comfortable as if you were in your bed.

"And it is time for you three to go to bed, too. Off with you: make haste!" So saying, he took the oil-lamp from the table, and went towards the kitchen. The three boys clattered along after him.

When he reached the door, he turned again and said, "There, sleep soundly. Must not think any more to-night, and it will be better for you by and by," and he went out. Presently his wife came into the room with an oil-lamp in her hand, and looked at the place where Wiseli was to sleep. "Can you lie there?" she asked. "You will find it warm enough by the stove. There are plenty of people who have neither bed nor a warm place to be in. You won't suffer in that way, and ought to be thankful that you are under a good roof. Good-night."

"Good-night," replied Wiseli, softly; but the woman could not have heard her, for she was already away when she spoke, and had closed the door behind her immediately. Now Wiseli sat alone in the dark room. Every thing about her was suddenly silent,--not a sound to be heard. A straggling moonbeam shone through the little window,--enough to show the child where the bench by the stove was, upon which she must find her bed. She crossed the room, and seated herself there. For the first time that day since she had left her dear mother, she found herself alone, and able to think over what had befallen her. She had been constantly under excitement until this moment; for every thing that had happened frightened her. All that she heard or saw since she left her home had been so very unpleasant that she could not stop to think at all, but went from one alarm to another. Now there she sat alone, without her mother, and began to realize that it was all over,--that they would never see nor hear each other again in this world. And such a sense of loneliness, of utter desolation, took possession of Wiseli, that she believed herself uncared for and forgotten by everybody, and feared that she should be left there alone to die in the dark. The poor child laid her head down upon her bundle, and began to cry, bitterly and despairingly, "Mother, can you not hear me? Mother, do not you hear me call?"

Now Wiseli's mother had often told her little girl, that when things went very badly with us here below, then was the moment to lift up our voices and cry to God for help; for he would hear us in our trouble when all other's ears were deaf, and help us when no other help was possible. At this moment the child remembered these words, and she sobbed aloud, "Oh, you dear God in heaven! help me also, I am so unhappy, and my mother cannot hear me when I call!"

And when she had prayed thus several times over, she felt calmer. It comforted her poor little heart; for now she felt that God was really there in heaven, and could help her, and that she was no longer alone. And presently she recalled her mother's words,--almost the very last that she spoke: "My child, when you cannot see your way clearly before you, and every thing seems strange and difficult"--And now it was so; and how little she thought that it ever would be so, when her mother was talking to her. Her mother told her to remember the words of the hymn,--

> "Your road He'll also find,
>   Nor let your footsteps stray."

Now Wiseli first rightly understood these words, and felt their full meaning. Before she had repeated them mechanically, for not until now did she need them. But it was just her present case. Was not she full of perplexity? and what could she possibly have in her cousin Gotti's house but fear and trouble? And so she repeated, again and again,--

"Your road He'll also find,
  Nor let your footsteps stray."

The child had found her way to her heavenly Father, and knew that he was sure to help her; and she felt comforted. Folding her little hands, she began the hymn at the beginning, for it seemed like talking to a kind friend; and she said each word from her very heart:--

"To God you must confide
Your sorrow and your pain;
He will true care provide,
And show you heaven again.
  "For clouds and air and wind
He points the path and way;
Your road He'll also find,
Nor let your footsteps stray."

A quiet trust now took possession of the child's heart. She fell asleep soon after, her head supported on her little bundle, still repeating the last lines of the hymn. And a pleasant dream followed. She saw before her a dry bright pathway in the full sunlight, and the road led between beautiful red roses and lovely pinks that were so attractive that she longed to run to gather them. And by her side stood her dear mother, and held her hand tenderly in her own, as she always did; and her mother pointed along the pathway in her dream, and said, "See, my Wiseli; did not I tell you so? That is your way."

"'Your road He'll also find,
  Nor let your footsteps stray.'"

And the child was happy in her dream, and slept as soundly on her little bundle as if she were on a soft bed.

CHAPTER V.
HOW TIME WENT ON, AND SUMMER CAME.

When old Trine carried the news back to the heights, and told them there that Wiseli's mother was dead, and the child taken at once to her cousin Gotti's, the whole family became greatly agitated. Mrs. Ritter could not cease bewailing her neglect in not visiting the sick woman before, for she had been postponing it from day to day; but, of course, had not in the least realized how near the end might be. She was sadly cast down, and sorrowful. And Otto: he went raging up and down the room with great strides, and kept calling out angrily, "It is an injustice! It is a great injustice! But if he dares to lay a hand on her to harm her, he may look to his own bones, how many of them will be left whole in his skin!"

"Who do you mean, Otto? Who are you talking about in that way?" said his mother, looking curiously at her excited boy.

"About that Cheppi," he replied. "I do not know what dreadful things he will do to Wiseli when he has her there in his own house. It is not right, but just let him try"--But now Otto was interrupted by a repeated and heavy stamping that prevented his being heard. "Why do you make such a deafening noise, you pussy cat, there behind the stove?" he cried, turning his indignation towards another quarter. Pussy came out from behind the stove, but stamped more violently than before; for she was trying to force her feet into her wet boots, which it had taken the old Trine ever so long to pull off a while before. It was dreadfully hard work; and Pussy became as red as fire, while she said,--

"Don't you see that I have to do so? Nobody in the world could get these boots on without stamping."

"And what in the world do you want to put those wet boots on again for? I have just pulled them off, so that you should not have them on. I should just like to know what this means?" said Trine, who stood looking on all this time.

"I am going to the beech grove this very minute to fetch Wiseli to our house. She can have my bed," said Pussy, decidedly. But quite as decidedly old Trine stalked over to Pussy, at these words, lifted her up, placed her firmly on a chair, while she pulled off the boot that was half on; but said, in a pacifying tone, to the kicking and excited child,--

"That is all right! that is all right! but I will take care of you first. You must not get two pair of shoes and two pair of stockings wet through in one day. You can give up your bed. You can go up into the lumber-room, if you want to: there is room enough there."

But Pussy had a very different plan in her little head. She thought that she could free herself, in this wise, of a great and daily recurring trouble, that often gave her both inward and outward annoyance; namely, the being ordered off to bed every evening, and obliged to go, into the bargain, just as she was in the mood to enjoy herself especially. She thought that, if she gave up her bed to Wiseli, there would be none other at hand for her, and so she could stay up as long as she wanted to.

She was so delighted at this prospect, that she did not, at first, notice how the sly Trine had wisked off her wet boots, and that now there was no chance to fetch Wiseli.

When she fairly understood how she had been tricked, she set up such an outcry that Otto put his fingers in his ears, and her mother came in, a good deal alarmed at the uproar. She promised Pussy to talk over the matter with her father as soon as he came home; for he had gone away that very morning, with their Uncle Max, to pay a long-promised visit to an old friend. After a while peace and quiet were restored in the household. The gentlemen did not return for two weeks, however; but Mrs. Ritter kept her promise. The first thing that she mentioned to her husband, on the very evening of his return, was the fact of Wiseli being an orphan, and her new shelter; and the colonel promised to go to the pastor the very next day, to see what better arrangement could be made for the child; and, having visited the pastor, the colonel brought back the sad news, that, on the Sunday just past, the parish had taken the matter into consideration, and that it was now settled. Wiseli must be housed somewhere; and, as her mother had not left any property whatever, she must also be maintained at the expense of the parish until she could support herself. Moreover, her cousin Gotti had offered, in the first instance, to take the child for a very slight compensation. He wished to do an act of charity as far as he could afford it. He was known to be a well-conducted man; and, as he made so slight a demand, it was agreed and settled that the child should henceforth find her home with him.

"It seems to me a very good arrangement," said the colonel to his wife. "The child will be well cared for there; besides, what else could be done? She is much too small to be placed anywhere in service, and certainly you cannot take every orphan child in the neighborhood into your own house. You might as well turn it into an asylum at once."

Mrs. Ritter was very much disturbed by the news that every thing had been settled so soon. She had hoped to be able to have found a different home for Wiseli, who was, she knew, much too sensitive and delicate a child to be happy in a home where rudeness and roughness were the rule; but she had not a definite plan in her mind, and now there was nothing to be done but to try to look after the child's comfort a little, and to protect her, if possible.

Otto and Pussy did not take the affair so quietly, however. They were in great excitement when they heard it all on the following morning.

Otto declared Wiseli's lot to be the lot of Daniel in the lion's den, and brought his fist down on the table with the evident wish that he were pommelling Cheppi's head. Pussy screamed, and cried a little; partly out of pity for Wiseli, and partly from disappointment that she could not now carry out her little plan of being able to sit up later in the evenings.

But this excitement was at last quieted down, like every other, by time; and the days rolled on in their wonted manner.

In the meantime Wiseli has become somewhat accustomed to the life in her cousin Gotti's house. For one thing, her bed had come; and she no longer slept on the bench by the stove, but in a little place partitioned off from the passage between her cousin's room and that of the boys. There was just room enough in this little place for her bed, and a little chest, in which she placed her clothes, and upon which she had to climb when she wished to get into her bed; for there was no space between.

She was obliged to go to the well when she washed; and, if it was very cold, then her cousin's wife said she could give up washing for that day, and do it on another when it was warmer. Now Wiseli was not used to this style of thing at all. Her mother had taught her that cleanliness was absolutely necessary; and Wiseli would have frozen rather than to look untidy, and, therefore, displease her mother. To be sure, every thing was different for her at home; for she washed and dressed herself in her mother's room always; and many a loving word they exchanged until the coffee was on the table, and they sat down together, and ate their breakfast happily, before Wiseli started off for school.

But what a difference for her now! All, all was changed,--her whole life from morning till evening; and often, at the thought of her mother, the tears started into the poor child's eyes, and her heart ached so sadly, that she felt as if she could go no farther, but must drop down, and die. But she held herself bravely, for it distressed her cousin Gotti to see her cry, and his wife scolded more than ever; for she, too, disliked to see her dull.

The happiest part of the twenty-four hours for Wiseli was when she climbed into her little bed at night, and had a moment's time to think about her dear mother in peace.

At this time she always obtained comfort. She thought about her beautiful dream, and felt perfect confidence that the good God would find a way for her out of her troubles, as her mother had told her; and she hoped that her mother was also in heaven, and would pray to God not to forget her poor little child left alone in the wide world. Then Wiseli always repeated her hymn, and slept quietly.

So the winter slipped away, and the spring with its sunshine followed. The trees were green again, and the meadows were gay with primroses and white anemones, and in the wood the cuckoo sang lustily; and soft, warm breezes were all abroad, making every heart beat more cheerily; and one rejoiced that life was still possible.

Wiseli also rejoiced over the flowers and the sunshine, especially when she went to and from school. Beyond this she had little time for enjoyment, for she had so much work to do. Every moment out of school she had to employ in some useful occupation; and, indeed, often was obliged to stay away from school for a half-day at a time, there was so much to be done that could not be neglected, as her cousin Gotti, and particularly his wife, were forever telling her. The cultivation of the fields had begun, and also the garden work; and when her cousin's wife was in the garden, then Wiseli had to wash the cooking utensils, and had the hogs' trough to cleanse and carry back to the barn; and then the boys' stockings and shirts must be mended, and her cousin's wife always said, "Oh, the child can do that, she has nothing else to do;" and yet she never was idle a single moment, and felt almost giddy at times, because she was called from one piece of work to another before she had time to breathe. Moreover, she found that if, for example, she ran over to the field with the seed-potatoes that her cousin Gotti was calling for, then his wife would scold because she had not made the kitchen-fire for the supper, as she was bidden to do; but if she stopped to make the fire, then she was found fault with by Cheppi because she had not mended the hole in his jacket-sleeve he had told her to long ago; and everybody called out, "Why don't you do this, or why don't you do that? you have nothing else to do." She was glad to go to school whenever she was allowed to go, for she was quiet for a while then; and, moreover, in that place the poor child heard a pleasant word now and again. For each time that recess came, or they left school to go home, Otto would come to her, and talk with her pleasantly for a while, or give her an invitation from his mother to visit them on Sunday evening and play games with the children. Poor Wiseli could never avail herself of these charming invitations, because on Sunday she had always to make the coffee for the family; and her cousin's wife said that she could not think of letting the child go away to visit on the only day when she was really of some use to her. But the child was glad that Otto always asked her, though she could not go, and that he always spoke kindly to her; for those were the only friendly acts or words that she knew of nowadays. There was still another reason that made it pleasant for Wiseli to go to school, and that was the passing by Andrew the carpenter's pretty garden on her way there. She always paused and looked over the low hedge, hoping that she might catch sight of the carpenter; for she had her mother's message to deliver, and never ceased hoping to find the opportunity. She was far too shy to go into the house for that purpose. She felt that she did not know Andrew well enough to venture to do that. She was particularly timid with him, because he was so very quiet, and always looked at her kindly when they met, but never spoke; or, at least, never said more than a kindly word in passing. And she had never succeeded in catching even a glimpse of him, no matter how long she stood by the hedge and looked over.

May passed, and June. The long days of summer came, with more and more work to be done in the fields, and work that was ever hotter and hotter. Wiseli felt this keenly when her cousin Gotti called her out to help with the haymaking, and the heavy rake was so hard for her to lift; or, worse still, to handle the clumsy wooden fork when the hay needed spreading in the sun to dry.

She often was obliged to work in the fields, and in the evening was so tired out that she could scarcely move her poor little arms. She never fretted, however, for she thought it was necessary and right; but often, when she was still for a moment in the evening, it hurt her sadly to hear Cheppi call out, "You ought to do your examples in arithmetic now, as I do. You are never doing any thing out of school, and in the classes you are always behind the others."

She would have liked to study and get on at her lessons, if she could only have gone regularly to school, and been able to keep up with the class. She was well aware that she was far behind her schoolmates; but what could she do, when she only got a little here and there, and all was confused for her, and she never knew what lessons were given out for the out-of-school studies. When she came quite unprepared to school, and could not answer the questions put to the class, she was overwhelmed with mortification, especially when the teacher would say, before all the other children, "I did not expect to see you so behindhand, Wiseli,--you of all others, who used to be so clever at your books." Then she used to feel fit to sink through the floor for shame, and would cry all the way as she walked home. But she did not dare to answer Cheppi back when he taunted her, because then he would begin to cry and scold, and make a noise, until his mother came in, when she, too, would reproach her with being behind her classes, because Cheppi said she was. So Wiseli often kept back her tears, and only gave way when she was alone; and sometimes it did seem to her as if she were quite forgotten by her heavenly Father and her mother, and as if nobody in the whole world cared for her; and she was too sad at heart even to say her comforting hymn for a long time; but she could not rest nor sleep until she had done so, even though there was little satisfaction for her in the words.

One beautiful evening in July Wiseli slept, after a sad time of weeping, and could not obtain an answer, the next morning, to her question of whether she might go to school with the boys.

Off scampered the boys. She looked sadly after them through the open window as they sprang away gayly through the flower-besprinkled grass, and chased a cloud of white butterflies along in front of them as they ran through the brilliant sunshine.

Her cousin's wife had prepared the big wash,--this was the work laid out for the whole week. Must Wiseli work there too?

Yes: already she heard a calling from the kitchen, and her cousin Gotti called her by name,--he stood at the well, and saw her looking out of the window.

"Make haste, make haste. Wiseli; it is time to be off: the boys are half-way to school. All the hay is in: make haste and go too." She did not wait till he told this twice. Like a flash she snatched her satchel and was off.

"Tell the teacher that I have not sent him his money for a long time, but he must not be vexed at that, we have had so much work with the hay this summer."

How happy the child felt as she flew along! She need not stand all day at the wash-tub: she could go instead to school. How beautiful it was everywhere about! The birds sang more sweetly than ever from the trees, the grass was scented, and the pretty red and yellow flowers glistened in the sun. Wiseli could not stop to enjoy them,--it was too late for that,--but she felt the beauty as she ran along, and rejoiced at every step.

That same evening, just as all the children streamed out of the close school-room into the beautiful afternoon light, the teacher called out, with his serious face peering into the little crowd, "Whose week is this?"

"Otto's, Otto's," called the whole company at once, and ran off.

"Otto," said the teacher, earnestly, "yesterday it was not swept up here at all. I excuse you for once; but do not let it happen again, or I must punish you, boy."

Otto looked for a moment at all the nut-shells and apple-parings and bits of paper that lay scattered about the floor waiting to be brushed up; then he turned his head quickly away, and scampered out of the door, for the teacher had disappeared into his own part of the house. Otto stood outside and gazed about him at the golden sunset, and thought, "If I could go home now, I could get a capful of cherries, and I could ride the brown horse home from the field when the groom fetches the hay; and now I must stay here instead, and sweep up these scraps from the floor!" And Otto was so angry over this unpleasant task, that he scowled about him, saying, "I wish the day of judgment would come, and carry off the schoolhouse, and break it up into a thousand pieces!" But every thing was still and peaceful all about, and not a sign of any such ravaging earthquake to be seen or heard.

After a while Otto turned back towards the schoolroom-door with a savage determination, for he knew that he must bite into his sour apple, or be punished the next day by having to sit still during recess; and he would not run the risk of that disgraceful punishment. He entered the room, but stood still with surprise as soon as he stepped past the threshold. Every thing was brushed up in the school-room: not a scrap nor bit to be seen anywhere. The windows all stood wide open, and the soft evening breeze blew through the quiet room. Just then the teacher came out of his own room and looked about him, and at the staring Otto, and said, pleasantly, "You may well look about you with satisfaction. I did not think that you could do it so well. You are a good scholar; but you have surpassed yourself to-day in cleaning up, for I never saw it so neatly done before."

So saying, the teacher went away; and after Otto had convinced himself by a last glance that what he saw was fact, and no witchcraft, he dashed down the steps, two at a time, across the little place and up the hillside: and not until he began to tell it all to his mother did he begin to wonder to whom he was indebted for this good turn.

"Nobody has done it through a mistake, that is certain," said his mother. "Have not you some good friend who is noble enough to sacrifice himself in this way for you? Think over all of them: who can it be?"

"I know," cried Pussy, who had been listening eagerly.

"Yes; pray who?" said Otto, half curiously, half incredulously.

"Jack, the mouse," explained Pussy in a tone of conviction; "because you gave him an apple last year."

"Oh, yes; or William Tell, because I did not take away his, year before last. One would be quite as probable as the other, you wonderfully clever Puss." And Otto ran away barely in time to catch the groom, who was going for the hay.

Wiseli also ran about this time. Down the hill with a happy heart and a merry countenance, past Andrew's garden, she ran, jumping and leaping in her frolicsome mood; and then about she went, and jumped back again to the garden, for she had espied the pinks all in bloom just within the enclosure, and must look at them again, they, were so beautiful. "I shall soon overtake the boys," she thought; "they stop at every corner to play ball."

But the pinks were most lovely to look upon; and they had such a sweet perfume, too, that the child lingered, looking over the low hedge for a long time. Suddenly Andrew came out of his house-door, and stood in front of Wiseli. He offered her his hand over the hedge, and said most kindly,--

"Will you take a pink, Wiseli?"

"Yes, indeed," she replied; "and I have a message to give you from my mother."

"From your mother?" repeated Andrew the carpenter in great surprise, and let the pink that he had just gathered fall from his hand. Wiseli ran round the hedge and picked it up from the ground; then she looked up at the man who stood still and looked at her strangely, and said,--

"Yes; at the very end, when my mother could do nothing more, she drank up the nice syrup that you put on the kitchen-table for her, and it refreshed her very much; and she charged me to tell you that she thanked you for it very much indeed, and for all the many acts of kindness that you had shown her; and she said, 'He always felt kindly to me.'"

Now Wiseli perceived that big tears rolled from Andrew's eyes and fell over his cheeks. He tried to say something, but could not speak. He pressed the child's hand, turned him about, and went into the house.

Wiseli stood still and wondered. Nobody had wept for her mother. Even she had not dared to cry, except when nobody could see her; for her cousin said that he would not have any whining, and she was even more afraid of making his wife angry. And now here was some one who wept because she had spoken of her mother to him. It seemed to the child as if Andrew were her very best friend upon the earth, and she felt herself strongly drawn towards him. But now she ran with her pink as fast as possible towards the beech grove; and it was well that she did so, for she saw the boys also drawing near the house, and it would never have done for her to be later than they.

Wiseli said her prayer with a light heart that night, and could not understand why she had been so depressed the night before, and why she had felt no confidence in God's kindness, and could not even say her hymn. Now she felt sure that he had not forgotten her, and she would never allow herself to think that again. Had she not received many kind things from him? And as she fell asleep she saw before her the kind face of Andrew the carpenter, with the tears in his eyes.

On the following day--it was Wednesday--Otto was again surprised by the good deed performed for him by his unknown friend; for he could not refrain from going out with the others when school was first over, and making a few gambols here and there to refresh himself after the long confinement. When, at last, he returned somewhat sadly to his work, it was all done again, and the schoolroom perfectly tidy. Now his curiosity began to be excited, and also gratitude to his invisible benefactor began to stir in his heart. He would certainly find out on Thursday what it all meant.

So, when the classes were dismissed, and they all left the house as usual, Otto stood for a while by his seat, thinking how he could discover his helpful friend. But a knot of his schoolmates rushed in as he stood there, grasped him by arms and shoulders, and dragged him out, crying, "Come along! Come on! We are playing 'Robbers,' and you must be our leader."

Otto defended himself for a moment. "This is my week," he cried.

"Oh, nonsense! put it off," they said. "Only just for a quarter of an hour. Come along!"

And Otto went. To tell the truth, he relied secretly upon his unseen friend, who would certainly shield him from punishment. He found it extremely agreeable to feel such a support under his feet; and the quarter slipped into the full hour, and Otto was lost. He went back to the schoolhouse to fulfil his duty, and threw open the door with such a slam that the master rushed out of his room very quickly, and asked,--

"What do you want, Otto?"

"Only to look in again, to see if every thing is as it should be," stammered the boy.

"This is excellent," said the teacher; "but it is not necessary for you to slam the door in that way."

Otto went away in good spirits. On Friday he made up his mind not to do his work of cleaning until he was satisfied about the mystery; and then,--then there would only be Saturday morning left of his week.

"Otto," called out the teacher on Friday, as the clock struck four, "take this paper over to the pastor as quickly as you can. He will give you some papers to bring back. It will only take you a moment or two, and you will be here in time to brush out the room."

The boy did not like to go very well, but there was no help for it; and, of course, he could be back in a twinkling. He reached the parsonage in half a dozen bounds. The pastor was busy, just then, with a visitor. His wife called Otto to her in the garden. She wanted to know how his mamma found herself; if his father were well, and Pussy, too; how Uncle Max was employed; and if they had good news from their relations in Germany. Then the pastor made his appearance, and Otto had to explain why it was his business to bring the papers, and what the teacher was doing at present. At last he got his papers, and was off like an arrow, pulled open the door of the schoolroom,--to find every thing swept and garnished, and no living being visible.

"And I have not been obliged to stoop once, to clear away the tiresome bits, the whole week through," thought Otto contentedly. "But who can have done all this dirty work without being obliged to do it?" Now he determined, for once and all, to have that question settled.

The school hours ended at eleven o'clock on Saturday. Otto waited until all the children had gone, and the room was empty. Then he went outside, closed the door, and leaned with his back against it. There could no one enter without his seeing who it was. He preferred to do this, rather than to go at once to work at the sweeping and cleaning. He waited and waited: no one came. He heard the clock strike the half-hour. There were plans at home for an excursion that afternoon. The family were to dine early, to get away soon after dinner. He ought to begin with his work at once, if he wanted to get home in good season. How he hated it!

He opened the door. Now Otto stared about him even more than he had done the first time. The work was all done. It was certainly so, and nicer than ever before.

Things began to look rather queerly to Otto. He thought of ghost stories, and such things. Very much more softly than usual he slipped out, and closed the door behind him. Just at the same time, something slipped silently out of the teacher's kitchen, and they came together face to face. It was Wiseli. She grew red and redder, just as if Otto had detected her in something mischievous. Now the truth flashed into his mind.

"So it is you who have done my work all the week, Wiseli?" he said. "Nobody else would have thought of doing it unless obliged to, I am sure of that."

"You have no idea how glad I am to get the chance," said Wiseli, in reply.

"No, no; you must not say that, Wiseli. Nobody in the world can be glad to do such things," said the boy decidedly.

"But I mean it,--I really do," repeated the girl. "I have thought, all day long through the week, with pleasure of the chance the afternoon would give me; and, while I was working, I was more than ever glad, because I thought, when Otto comes, he will find the work done, and be pleased."

"But what put it into your head to do it for me?"

"Oh! I knew how much you disliked it; and I have always wanted to give you something, as you once gave me your sled. Don't you remember? But I have nothing to give."

"What you have done is worth a great deal more than lending a sled. I won't forget your kindness, Wiseli." So saying, Otto offered her his hand, quite overcome for the moment.

Wiseli's eyes shone with satisfaction as they seldom did nowadays. Presently Otto wanted to know how she had managed to get into the room again, for he had always waited until all the children were gone.

"Oh! I never did go out," said the girl. "I hid myself quickly behind the closet-door. I thought you would go out for a few moments, as usual."

"How did you get out without my seeing you afterwards?" Otto wanted to know all about it.

"Oh! while you were running around with the other boys, I got out easily enough. I listened; but yesterday and to-day, as I was not certain where you were, I went through the teacher's kitchen, and asked his wife if she had any errand for me to do,--she often gives me a message to carry somewhere,--and then I went out that way. Yesterday I was behind the kitchen-door when you ran into the school-room."

Now Otto knew all the ghost story. He offered his hand again to Wiseli. "I thank you," he said; and they both ran off with happy hearts, each a separate way.

CHAPTER VI.
OLD AND NEW.

Summer was over, and Autumn had followed in her footsteps. The evenings were cool and misty. In the damp meadows the cows were eating the last grass of the season, and here and there little fires were visible where the sheep-boys cooked their potatoes and warmed their stiffened fingers.

It was on such a misty evening that Otto, on leaving the schoolhouse, ran home for a moment to tell his mother that he was going to see what kept Wiseli from school; for she had not been there since the autumn vacation,--certainly not for eight days.

As he approached the beech grove, he saw Rudi sitting before the door, eating pear after pear from a heap that lay before him.

"Where is Wiseli?" asked Otto.

"Outside," was the answer.

"Where outside?"

"In the meadow."

"In which meadow?"

"I don't know;" and Rudi went on munching his pears.

"You won't die early because you know too much," remarked Otto, and went haphazard towards the big meadow that stretched away from the house to the wood.

Presently he discovered three black spots under the pear-trees, and went towards them.

He was right. There was Wiseli stooping over the pears which she was sorting, while a little farther off Cheppi sat astride of his rake; and behind him Harnes lay on his back across the piled-up basket, and rocked it back and forth so violently, that it nearly fell over at each movement. Cheppi looked at him, laughing loudly.

When Wiseli saw Otto coming towards her, her whole countenance glowed with pleasure.

"Good evening, Wiseli," cried the lad from afar. "Why have you not been to school for so long?"

The girl stretched out her hand with a pleasant smile to her friend.

"We have had so much to do that I was not able to go," she said. "Just look, what a lot of pears we have! I have to sort them from morning till night, there are so many."

"Your shoes and stockings are all wet. It is not pleasant here. Are you not cold when you are so wet?"

"Yes, I do feel chilly sometimes; but, in general, I get very warm at this work."

At this moment Hannes gave his basket such a powerful twist that over it went, and there lay Hannes, the basket, and the pears all in a heap on the ground.

"Oh, oh!" cried Wiseli in distress; "now they are all to be picked up again."

"And this one, too," cried Cheppi, and laughed aloud as the pear that he had in his hand struck Wiseli's cheek with such force that it brought the tears to her eyes, and she turned quite white with the pain.

Scarcely had Otto seen this than he flew at Cheppi, threw him and his rake to the ground, and seized him by the nape of the neck.

"Stop, or I shall choke!" Cheppi was not laughing now.

"I want to make you remember that you will also have me to deal with in future, when you treat Wiseli in that way," said Otto, scarlet with anger. "Have you got enough? Will you remember it now?"

"Yes, yes! Let me go!" said Cheppi, in a very humble tone.

Otto released him.

"Now you have felt," he said, "how it will be whenever you hurt Wiseli again. I will give you some more of this each time, even if you are sixty years old. Good-by, Wiseli." And Otto went his way to carry his anger to his mother.

He unburdened himself to her as soon as he reached home. It was a terrible thing to the generous boy that Wiseli should be obliged to submit to such treatment. He was determined to go at once to the pastor to complain of him and of his whole family, and demand that Wiseli should be taken away from them at once. His mother listened quietly to him, and let his indignation have time to cool off a little; then she said,--

"I do not think, my dear boy, that there is the least use in your doing this.

They would not take the child from her cousin Gotti, I am sure; and it would only irritate him, should he hear that such a thing was thought of. He himself does not feel unkindly towards Wiseli, and there is really no sufficient ground for removing her from his roof. I know very well that the poor girl has a hard time of it there. I have not forgotten her, and am constantly hoping to find some way to help her. It lies very heavily on my heart to know how much she has to suffer, you may be sure of that, Otto. And if you can at any time manage to shelter her and intimidate that brutal fellow Cheppi, without being too rough yourself, I shall be very glad."

Otto took what comfort he could in the knowledge that his mother was constantly looking out for some way to help Wiseli.

He was always planning some way to help her himself, but never hit upon any thing that could be carried out. He saw very well that she could not free herself; and the only idea that occurred to him as Christmas drew near was to write on his list of wishes, in huge letters so big that they could easily be read from heaven above, "I wish that the Christ child would set Wiseli at liberty."

Winter was come again, and the coast offered its feast of inexhaustible pleasure to the children, who never wearied of its charm. The moon shone with the most unusual brightness, it seemed to Otto, who, at last, had the cleverness to suggest that all the children should collect on the hillside at seven o'clock to take advantage of its beauty for an evening coasting-party.

This suggestion was received with universal approbation, and the children separated at five o'clock when it began to be dark, to meet again at seven for their favorite amusement.

Otto's mother was not so enthusiastic over this great scheme as were the children, and could not agree with them when they expressed their delight. She said it was too cold for them to be out late into the evening; that there was great danger of accidents in the uncertain moonlight; and particularly objected to allowing Pussy to expose herself. But her objections only served to enhance the interest the children felt for the expedition, and Pussy pleaded for her consent as if her very life hung on being one of this coasting-party. Otto promised, "upon his word of honor," that he would not let any thing happen to his sister, and would always keep near to her and protect her. At last their mother gave her consent; and, with great noise and rejoicing, the children went out into the beautiful, clear, cold moonlight.

Every thing went on without a drawback. The coast was in perfect condition; and the mysteriousness of the darker places, upon which the moonlight did not fall, heightened the interest of the occasion. There were a vast number of children assembled, and all were in the best humor. Otto let them all go down first; then he followed, and Pussy came last of all, so that no one could run her down. Otto had arranged it in this way, so that he could always glance backward to see that his little sister went safely down the coast.

As every thing went so smoothly and happily, somebody proposed that they should make a "train;" that is, bind all the sleds together, and so go down: it would be more delightful than ever by moonlight. No sooner said than done. Only Pussy's sled was not tied to her brother's, for he feared lest the straining and shocks that often took place in this kind of coasting might prove dangerous to her. She followed, therefore, as usual; but Otto could not stop his sled if she was delayed, for he had to go on with the "train." Off they went, and the long chain reached the bottom safely and happily.

Suddenly Otto heard a fearful cry, and he recognized at once his little sister's voice. What had happened? He had no choice, however, but to go down to the very end with the merry party to which he was closely fastened--down to the foot of the hill, no matter how great his fear might be. Once at the bottom, however, he tore his sled loose, and ran up the hill as quickly as possible, with all the others at his heels; for they had all heard the screams, and wanted to see what they meant. Half-way up the ascent stood Pussy by her sled, and screamed and cried rivers of tears. Out of breath with his haste, Otto could hardly call out, "What is the matter? What has happened?"

"He did--he did--he did," sobbed Pussy, and could get no further.

"What did he do? Who was it? Where? Who?" stammered Otto.

"That man there, that man; he did try to kill me, and said terrible words, too."

As much as this Otto understood, accompanied by screams and sobs.

"Be quiet now, Pussy: do not go on like that. He did not kill you, after all. Did he really strike you?" asked Otto, very gently and soothingly, for he was much alarmed.

"No," sobbed Pussy, beginning again; "but he was going to. He had a stick, and he held it out like that, and said, 'Wait a moment;' and such dreadful words he said, too."

"Then he really did not do any thing to hurt you?" asked Otto, and began to breathe more freely.

"But he did, he did; and you were all off down the hill, and I was all alone." And Pussy's tears and sobs continued to break forth.

"Hush, hush!" said Otto, consolingly. "Now try to be quiet. I will not leave you again, and the man will not trouble you any more; and if you will be quiet and good, I will give you the red candy cock that was on the Christmas-tree."

This made an impression upon Pussy. She dried her eyes, and did not make another sound; for that big red candy cock on the Christmas-tree was what the child had most wished for. In the division of the things it had fallen to Otto's share; but his little sister had never forgotten her longing for it. Now that every thing was quiet again, the children began to climb the hill, and they tried to make out who the man could be who had threatened to kill Pussy.

"Oh, kill! Not so bad as that," interposed Otto. "I saw a big man with a stick, who was obliged to step into the snow to get out of our way when we went down the coast on the 'train.' It made him angry to be obliged to go into the snow; and finding Pussy alone there, he scolded her a little to relieve himself."

This explanation satisfied everybody, it was so perfectly natural. Everybody wondered that they had not thought of it before,--indeed, thought they had,--and soon forgot all about it, and continued coasting. This, however, had an end, like all other pleasures; for eight o'clock had struck long ago, and that was the hour at which they were to break up and go home. On the way back, Otto charged Pussy not to speak of her adventure; otherwise their mother would never again let them go coasting in the moonlight. She should have the candy cock, but must promise not to say a word if she took it.

All traces of her tears had long vanished, and nothing betrayed their secret to the family.

Both children slept quietly in their beds soon after, and Pussy dreamed of the red candy cock, and shouted out with pleasure in her dreams. Presently there was a loud knocking at the house-door, that made Colonel Ritter and his wife spring up from the table, where they were comfortably talking about the children; and old Trine called out of the window, in an angry tone,--

"What sort of a way of knocking is that?"

"A terrible thing has happened," said some one from below. "We want the colonel to come down the hill. They have found Andrew the carpenter dead." And off ran the messenger again.

Mr. and Mrs. Ritter had heard enough, however, for they had heard this sad news from the window. The colonel threw his cloak about his shoulders, and hastened down to the carpenter's. As he entered the room, he found that there were already a crowd of people assembled. The justice of the peace and the chief magistrate had been fetched, and a number of curious and sympathetic people had come along with them. Andrew lay on the floor, in his blood, and gave no sign of life. The colonel went to his side.

"Has nobody been for the doctor?" he asked. "We want a doctor at once."

Nobody had thought of that,--there was no use in trying to do any thing, they said.

"Run, somebody, as quickly as possible," said the colonel. "Go, you,"--to a lad who stood near,--"tell the doctor that I send him word to come here immediately." He helped to raise Andrew from the ground, and to carry him into his bedroom, and to lay him on the bed. Then he went back to the chattering group of neighbors, to find out how the accident had taken place,--if anybody knew the precise circumstances.

The miller's son stepped forward, and told his story. He was passing the house about a half-hour ago, he said; and, seeing a light in the window, stopped to ask if his bits of furniture were finished. He found the door of the room open, and Andrew lying dead on the floor, covered with blood; and by his side stood Meadow-Joggi, and held out a piece of gold between his fingers. Then the miller's son had called all the neighbors, and sent some one for the chief magistrate and everybody whose business it was.

Meadow-Joggi--who was so called because he lived down in the meadow-land--was a foolish fellow, who was supported by the neighbors, who gave him little jobs of work suitable to his feeble capacity, such as carrying sand or stone where they were needed, or helping to sort the fruit, or gathering fagots in winter.

No one ever had heard of his doing any mischief. The miller's son told him to stay where he was until the president came; and so Joggi stood in the corner, held his fist tightly closed, and laughed to himself. The doctor soon arrived on the scene, and behind him came the president. The council took its place in the middle of the room, to consider the case. The doctor, however, went at once into the bedroom, and the colonel followed him. The doctor examined the motionless body carefully.

"Here it is," he cried presently. "Here, at the back of the head, is where Andrew was struck. There is a large wound here."

"But he is not dead, doctor, is he?"

"No, no; he breathes feebly, but it is with difficulty."

The doctor wanted all sorts of things,--water and sponges, and linen rags, and so on,--and the people ran this way and that, and searched and pulled things out from the closets and drawers, and produced a heap of things, but nothing that was useful for this occasion.

"We want a woman here who has some intelligence, and knows what is needed in sickness," said the doctor at last, rather impatiently. They all called out this one or that one; but not one was able to come of all those mentioned.

"Let somebody go to the 'Heights,' and tell my wife to send old Trine down here," said the colonel. And somebody ran off.

"Your wife won't thank you," said the doctor; "for I shall not be able to let the nurse leave this patient for three days and nights."

Trine came, laden with all needful things, much sooner than anybody dared hope for her; for she was all ready with her big basket packed, and her mistress stood by her side, expecting the order for her to go down to Andrew's; for they would not believe that Andrew was dead, and had thought of every thing that could possibly be needed. She had sponges and bandages, lint and oil, and warm flannels, packed in her basket, and had only to run off when the messenger came. The doctor was delighted.

"Everybody must go now. Good-night, colonel; and turn all those people out of the house, will you?" cried the doctor, and closed the door without ceremony as soon as the colonel went out.

The committee was still sitting, but the colonel explained that the house must be emptied; so they decided to imprison Joggi, and then institute investigations. Two men took Joggi between them, so that he could not get away, and carried him off to the poor-house, and shut him up in a room. Joggi went with them very willingly, and laughed now and then, and looked into his hand.

The following morning Mrs. Ritter hastened down to Andrew's house in great anxiety. Trine came softly from the bedroom, and brought the welcome news that Andrew had come to himself a little; that the doctor had already made his visit, and found his patient in better condition than he expected; but he left especial orders that nobody should be allowed to enter the room. Andrew was not to be permitted to speak one word, even if he wished to speak: only the doctor and the nurse might come into his presence. Trine said these words with great pride, for she was a very good nurse, and well aware of the importance of the situation. Mrs. Ritter fully appreciated all this, and went home rejoicing over the news.

A week went by. Every morning Mrs. Ritter went down to the sick man's house to obtain an accurate statement of his condition herself, and to find out if any thing were needed for his comfort, in order that all his wants might be supplied at once. Every day Otto and Pussy sent the same message; namely, "When could they be permitted to see their sick friend?" but the doctor was inexorable. There was no possibility of Trine being allowed to go, either; and the doctor could not praise her enough for her intelligent care of the patient. After the week was fairly over, however, the doctor sent word to the colonel that if he would come to Andrew's at the same time he made his daily visit, they would go in together; for now that Andrew was able to talk, the doctor wished to have the colonel hear what could be told about the terrible assault that had prostrated the good carpenter.

Andrew was very glad to press the colonel's hand gratefully in his own,--he knew very well where all the care and comfort came from with which he was surrounded.

He collected his thoughts to the best of his ability to answer the questions put to him. This was, however, all that he could tell them. He had taken out the yearly sum of money that he always carried up to the colonel for investment, and was in the act of counting it over once again, to be sure that it was right. It was rather late in the evening, and he was seated with his back towards the door. While he was in the midst of counting, he heard some one enter the room; and before he had time to turn about, he received a tremendous blow upon his head. After that, all was a blank.

There had been a heap of money upon the table. Nothing was to be found of it, however, but the piece that Joggi held in his hand when they found him.

Even supposing that Joggi were the malefactor, where was the rest of that money? When Andrew learned that they had taken Joggi into custody and shut him up, he was very uneasy.

"Oh, you must let him go, poor Joggi!" he said. "He never would hurt the smallest infant. *He* never struck me."

For all that, Andrew had no suspicion who it could have been. He had no enemy, he said, and knew of nobody who would wish him harm.

"It may have been a stranger," suggested the doctor, as he looked at the window. "If you sat here, with the bright light shining upon your pile of money while you counted it over on the table, anybody going by the house could have seen you, and taken a notion to rob you."

"I suppose it must have been in that way," said Andrew. "I never thought of such a thing, however. Every thing has always stood open in the house."

"It is well that you have laid something by already, Andrew," said the colonel. "Do not fret over this: it is so lucky that you will soon be well again."

"Certainly, colonel; and I have every reason for thankfulness. The good God has given me far more than I have any use for." And he shook hands with his friends, who agreed, in parting, that Andrew was much less to be pitied than the man who tried to kill him.

There was a sad story told about Joggi, which excited the sympathy of the schoolboys exceedingly. Otto brought it home with him and repeated it several times, for it made a deep impression on his mind. It seemed that when they brought Joggi, laughing all the way, into the almshouse that evening, he was told to give up his piece of gold to one of his guards,--the son of the justice of the peace; but Joggi shut his fist tighter, and would not give it up at all. But the two men were stronger than he, and at last forced his hand open; and, as they took the money away from him, one of them said, "Only wait a little till the others come, then you will get what you deserve. You will see!" For he was vexed at the scratches he had got in the struggle.

These threats had frightened the poor half-witted fellow, who thought he was going to be beheaded, having no idea of what his punishment might be. And he refused to eat, and cried and groaned incessantly.

The officers of justice had been to see him twice, to assure him that, if he would only tell them what he had done, he should not be punished. He repeated that he had not done any thing but look in at the window; and when he saw Andrew on the floor, he went to him and shook him a little, and then he was dead. He saw something shining in the corner, and picked it up; and then the miller's son came in, and a lot of other people.

When Joggi got thus far in his story, he began to cry and groan, and would not be pacified.

CHAPTER VII.
ANDREW IS BETTER, AND
SOMEBODY ELSE, ALSO.

Mrs. Ritter went, as usual, to visit her friend, but no longer remained closeted with Trine, for she could now go freely into his room, talk with him for a little while, and mark his daily improvement. Otto and Pussy also paid several visits, armed with dainties for their favorite. So that Andrew said to the old Trine, with great feeling, "If I were a king, they could not show me more kindness."

The doctor was well pleased with the rapidity of the cure, and said to the colonel, whom he met on the threshold one day,--

"Every thing has worked wonderfully well. Your wife can have her Trine back again; and tell her she was worth her weight in gold. I only wish there were some one to stay with Andrew for a little while; or who could come in, now and then, to help him. The poor fellow must have something to eat, and he has no wife nor child,--in fact, nobody. Do ask Mrs. Ritter if she cannot think of something that will help us."

The colonel carried his message correctly, and his wife went the next day to Andrew's, as usual; and, seating herself by his bedside, said, without circumlocution, "I have something to say to you, Andrew. Are you inclined to listen to me?"

"Certainly, certainly. Every thing you do is right," said Andrew, supporting his head on his hand, and prepared to give her all his attention.

"I am going to take Trine away, now that you are so well," began Mrs. Ritter.

"Oh, dear lady, I beg you to believe me, I have wished to send her home for a long time past. I know how much you must miss her."

"I would not have allowed her to enter my house, if she had tried to come back before," replied Mrs. Ritter. "But now it is different: the doctor has dismissed her. He says, however,--and I fully agree with him,--that you need some one who can wait upon you, cook for you, or fetch your food from my house, and do a hundred little things: somebody for at least a few weeks. Now, Andrew, why cannot you have little Wiseli to do this?"

The words were scarcely spoken, when Andrew almost sprang up in his bed.

"No, no, Mrs. Ritter; certainly not!" he said, and became very red from excitement. "I could not dream of such a thing. Could I lie here in bed, and let that delicate little thing work for me out there in the kitchen? Oh! in Heaven's name, how could I think of her poor mother, where she lies buried? How she would look at me, if she knew of my doing such a thing. No, no, Mrs. Ritter; I would rather not get well at all."

Mrs. Ritter did not try to stop him; but, when he sunk back again upon his pillow, she said quietly,--

"It is not any thing very shocking, however, that I have proposed, Andrew: think it over now. You know what kind of care Wiseli is getting, do you not? Do you suppose she has nothing to do there, or even light work suitable to her strength? Hard work she has, and hard words with it. Would you give her any thing like that? Do you know what the child's mother would do, if she were standing here by our side? She would thank you, with tears in her eyes, if you would take her child into your house, where she could be happy. I am sure of that. And you would soon see how useful she would make herself."

After these touching words, Andrew began to take another view of the matter. He wiped his eyes, and said softly, "How can I be sure that the child would be willing? And how can I get her? Her cousin would not wish to part with her, probably."

"That is all right. You need not trouble yourself about that, Andrew," said his friend, cheerfully, as she rose to go. "I will attend to it all for you. It is a thing about which I have thought long and anxiously."

She took her leave; but, as she was passing out of the door, Andrew called out again,--

"Only in case Wiseli herself is perfectly willing: you will not forget that, please, Mrs. Ritter."

She promised again that the child should come gladly, or not at all, and left the house.

She went down the hill at once to the beech grove, for she was impatient to take Wiseli where she could think of her in safety. She met the cousin Gotti just as he was himself entering his own house. He saluted her, without concealing his surprise at her visit. But she did not leave him in doubt for a moment over the object that brought her there, and how anxious she was that Wiseli should take charge of the wounded Andrew at once, as she was sure she could do, if they were willing. His wife, who was in the kitchen, came directly she heard their voices, and was at once informed of Mrs. Ritter's proposition. But she answered that it was not possible, for the child was not able to be of use to anybody. But her husband interposed. The truth should be told: Wiseli was able and willing to work, and did so, well and intelligently. He did not wish to have her go, for she was useful and obedient. He would not refuse, for two weeks or so, to let her nurse Andrew. He would not probably need her longer than that, and then she must come back; for there was a great deal of work on hand against the spring.

"Yes, yes," said his wife. "I have no mind to begin it all over again teaching her, it has given me so much trouble already. If Andrew wants anybody to help him, let him get somebody for himself."

"Well, well; for two weeks, as I have promised, she shall go. It is our duty to help a neighbor, if we can."

"I thank you for your kindness," said Mrs. Ritter, rising. "And Andrew will himself show his gratitude. May I take Wiseli with me at once?"

Although his wife grumbled out that there could not be any such hurry, her husband said it was better the child should go at once. The sooner she went, the more quickly she would be back again; and repeated that it was only for fourteen days in all.

Wiseli was called, and told to get her clothes together, and tied in a bundle. The child obeyed, not daring to ask for a reason. It was exactly a year since she had brought the little bundle into the house. Nothing had been added to her scanty wardrobe in that time but a black frock. She wore that now, but it had been so long in use, that it hung about her almost in rags; and Wiseli looked shyly at Mrs. Ritter as she stood before her now, with her little bundle on her arm. The colonel's wife understood the look, and answered it. "Come, my dear; we are not going far away. You can go as you are."

Quickly taking leave, she waited only for Wiseli to give her cousin Gotti her hand. He said,--

"Oh, you are soon coming back; this is not a separation."

Off trotted Wiseli in silence, and much astonished, behind Mrs. Ritter, who walked rapidly across the snow-covered fields, as if she feared they both might be recalled; but as soon as they were out of sight of the beech grove, she turned about, and stood still. "Wiseli," she said kindly, "do you know Andrew the carpenter?"

"Certainly, I do," said the child; and glanced at her friend with such a happy expression, that Mrs. Ritter was rather surprised.

"He is ill," she proceeded. "Would you like to take care of him, and wait upon him a little, for about two weeks?"

"Yes, indeed!" replied the child promptly; and her face, that became suddenly rosy with pleasure, told Mrs. Ritter more than her short answer.

The good lady was pleased, but did not understand the child's feeling, for she knew nothing of her gratitude for Andrew's kindness to her mother. After they had gone on a while, Mrs. Ritter said,--

"You can tell Andrew the carpenter that you are very glad to go to take care of him, or he will not believe it. Don't forget to tell him that."

"No, no; I won't forget," said Wiseli. "I was just thinking about it myself."

They reached the house at last. Mrs. Ritter told Wiseli to go in alone, promising to come down in the morning to see how things went on; and, if she needed any thing for her patient, she could come up to the "Heights" to fetch it herself.

Wiseli stole into the garden, and opened the house-door. She knew that Andrew lay within in the bed-room behind the sitting-room. She entered the room softly. No one was there; but it was in good order, as old Trine had left it when she went away.

The child looked about to see that every thing was in the right place. Against the wall, in the back part of the room, stood a big wooden bedstead called a coach, and which was all arranged like a proper bed. The curtain was almost closed across it, but Wiseli could see how neat and clean it looked, and wondered who slept there usually. Presently she knocked quietly at the bedroom door; and when Andrew called out, "Come in," she entered, and shyly stood before him. Andrew raised himself in his bed to see who was there.

"Oh, oh!" he said, partly glad and partly startled. "Is that you, Wiseli? Come here; give me your hand." The child obeyed.

"You did not come to me against your will?"

"No, no," replied the child; "surely not." But Andrew was not satisfied.

"I mean, Wiseli," he continued, "perhaps you would have liked better not to come; but perhaps you wanted to do a kindness to the good colonel's wife, she is so kind."

"No, no," repeated the child again; "she did not say any thing to me about it being for her. She only asked me if I was willing to go to you, and there is nobody in all the world to whom I would go so gladly as to you."

These words must have quieted all Andrew's scruples, for he did not ask any more questions, but let his head sink back on his pillow, and lay gazing silently at Wiseli; and presently he turned his head aside, and wiped his eyes several times.

"What shall I do now?" asked Wiseli, as Andrew did not move his head. He turned at the sound of her voice, and said, very kindly, "I do not know, I am sure, Wiseli. You may do any thing that you like, if you will only stay with me a little while."

Wiseli scarcely knew what to think. Since the death of her mother, nobody had spoken to her in such kindly, loving tones. It seemed as if her mother's voice and love were come into Andrew's words and tones. She took his hand in both hers, as she often took her mother's, and stood by the bedside. She did not even speak, but felt that her mother's loving presence was about them. Andrew, too, had a silent, peaceful conviction that Wiseli's mother was happy in their happiness.

Presently Wiseli said, "I think I ought to cook something for you: it is past twelve o'clock already. What shall I cook?"

"Whatever you like," said Andrew. But Wiseli knew that she was there for the purpose of making things comfortable for the sick man, and she did not cease her questioning until she found out what he usually had to eat,--a good nourishing soup, and a piece of the meat that was in the closet; and then Andrew said she must cook something with milk for herself.

The child was perfectly at home in the kitchen. She had really learned a great deal at her cousin Gotti's, even if she had received many cross words at the same time. She had every thing ready in a short time; and Andrew begged her to push a little table to the bedside, and sit down and eat with him, so that he could enjoy the pleasure of her company. Neither Wiseli nor Andrew had eaten such a pleasant meal for a long, long time. After eating, Wiseli rose; but Andrew looked at her sadly, and said, "Where are you going now, Wiseli? Won't you stay with me here a little longer, or is it too dull for you?"

"No, indeed, not dull; but after dinner the things must be washed and put away in their places in good order," said the child.

"I know," said Andrew; "but I thought that just for to-day--the first day, you know--you might put them away as they are, and to-morrow wash them all together."

"But if the colonel's wife should see them so, I should almost die of shame;" and Wiseli looked very grave while she spoke.

"Yes, yes; you are right," said Andrew. "Do whatever you think best."

So the child went to work, and cleaned and sorted and swept, so that every thing shone in the kitchen. Then she stood quietly, and looked on her work with satisfaction, saying softly, "Now Mrs. Ritter may come when she will."

Going into the room next the kitchen, she cast an admiring glance at the beautiful big bed on the "coach" behind the curtain; for Andrew the carpenter had told her that she was to sleep there, and that the little chest of drawers in the corner was also for her, and that she might put all her things there, if she liked.

So she laid away all the clothes in her little bundle in good order; but it did not take long to do that, they were so few. At last she returned to Andrew, and seated herself by his bedside. He had been looking towards the door very wistfully for a long time. She had scarcely seated herself before she asked, "Have not you a stocking to be knitted, or something else for me to do?"

Wiseli had been well drilled,--first by her mother, and then by her cousin's wife, whose words she never forgot, they frightened her so; and when Andrew said,

"Oh, you have worked enough for to-day; let us sit still and talk over all sorts of things together now," the child replied, "I do not like to sit and do nothing, for it is not Sunday; but we can talk while I knit, you know."

Andrew was pleased at this sign of the little girl's industry, and he again bade her do whatever she thought right and best. She might get a stocking to knit, if she wanted to: he had not one for her, however.

So Wiseli fetched her own, and took her seat by the bedside; and, truly, she could talk and knit at the same time perfectly well.

Andrew chose the one subject for their conversation that was by far the most agreeable to Wiseli; namely, her mother. It was the first time she had been able to talk about her mother to anybody since her death. But now she had a listener who could not hear enough, and so she told all that she could remember of their happy life together.

And day after day slipped by. For every little thing that Wiseli did, Andrew thanked her over and over,--not from politeness or mere form, but because every thing pleased the good man, and he wanted to express his pleasure. He became strong and well very rapidly under Wiseli's care, and soon was able to leave his bed. And the doctor was much surprised to see how quickly his strength had returned, and how happy he looked besides. He sat at the window in the sunshine all day long, and watched Wiseli as she moved about, as if he could never get enough of her. His eyes followed her as she went here to a drawer, opened it and shut it again; and noticed how every thing that passed through her hands was done in an orderly, regular manner, such as he had never seen before. And Wiseli was so happy, so happy, in this quiet little house, where she never heard any but loving words, and moved constantly in an atmosphere of affection, that made it impossible for her to allow her thoughts to dwell on the sad fact that the fourteen days would soon be past, and then she must return to the beech grove.

CHAPTER VIII.
SOMETHING VERY STRANGE HAPPENS.

On the "Heights" there was a great deal of talk about Andrew and Wiseli. Mrs.

Ritter went down every day, and always brought back good accounts. They all rejoiced together over this, and Otto and Pussy formed a plan to have a great convalescence festival in Andrew the carpenter's room while Wiseli was still with him. It should be a great surprise for them both. But before that came another feast,--their father's birthday. And the children had invented all sorts of "celebrations" from early morning on, but the great moment was yet to come; namely, at dinner-time. Otto and Pussy had taken their seats, full of excitement and expectancy.

The father and mother made their appearance, and the merriment began.

After one or two surprises came a large covered dish,--certainly that was a birthday dish. The cover was removed, and, behold, a beautiful cauliflower!

"This is a fine vegetable," said the father; "I must admire it. But, to tell the truth," he went on, with an air of disappointment, "I expected something different. I expected artichokes. They are to be found and bought as well as cauliflowers. You know, my dear Mary, there is no dish I care for so much as artichokes."

Suddenly Pussy called out,--

"That is it! that is it! That is exactly what he called to me twice. And he raised his stick in the air, and did so,"--and Pussy raised her arm in the air in great excitement. But suddenly she was quiet, and put her arm under the table, and turned crimson; and Otto, who sat on the other side of the table, looked at her with flashing eyes and very angry looks.

"What is this?" asked the colonel. "A strange way to celebrate my birthday. My daughter cries out, on one side, as if some one were going to kill her; and, on the other, my son is giving me such kicks on the shin that I shall soon be covered with black-and-blue spots. I should like to know where you learned this agreeable amusement, Otto?"

Now it was Otto's turn to become fiery red. His intention had been to give Pussy certain decided warnings to keep quiet, but his boot had encountered his father's leg instead, and not gently either. When he discovered his mistake, he did not dare to raise his eyes.

"Now, Pussy," said the colonel, "tell me the end of your robber story. You said the terrible man called out 'artichokes' to you, and raised his stick in the air; and then"--

"Then--then," stammered Pussy, who perceived that she had betrayed every thing, and would have to give the sugar cock back to Otto again. "Then he did not strike me, or kill me."

"Well, that was nice of him," said her father, laughing. "And what else?"

"Nothing else," said Pussy, whimpering.

"Well, then, the story had a good ending. The stick remained in the air, and Pussy came back to the house like an 'artichoke.' Now we will drink the health of the 'artichokes' and of Andrew the carpenter together."

The father raised his glass, and his companions did the same. When they left the table, they were all rather sad; all except the father, who took his newspaper, and lighted his cigar, as usual. Otto stayed in another room in the corner, and thought how, when the children were all allowed to go again to coast by moonlight, he would be obliged to remain at home; for his mother would not now let him go, he was sure. Pussy crept into her bedroom, nestled down in a corner by the bed upon a footstool, took the red candy cock upon her lap, and felt very sadly at the thought that she held it for the last time.

At the window her mother stood sadly thinking. She soon became agitated, however, and moved uneasily about the room, and presently began to seek for her little daughter in every corner. She found her at last, in her hiding-place behind the bed, sunk in deep dejection.

"Pussy," said her mother, "I want you to tell me the story about the man who threatened you. When was it, and where, and what words did he use?"

Pussy told all that she knew, but did not give much more information than she had conveyed at the table. The man had called out the same word that her father had used at table,--that she was sure of. Her mother turned away, went directly to the room where her husband was smoking, and said, in a very excited tone, "I must tell you, for I am more and more sure of it."

The colonel put down his newspaper and looked at his wife, much surprised.

"That scene at table has made me think of something; and the more I think, the surer I am about it."

"Do sit down, and tell me what you mean," said the colonel, who now became very curious. His wife did as he desired, and went on.

"You noticed Pussy's excitement. She must have been very much frightened by the man of whom she spoke. She was not joking. Therefore it is clear to my mind that the word was not 'artichoke,' but 'aristocrat,' that he used. Now you know who used to call us that,--my brother and I. Pussy has just told me that this took place on that evening when they all went coasting by moonlight; and that was the night when Andrew was assaulted and robbed. That rascally fellow Jorg has not been seen for years in this vicinity; and the very first time that there is any trace of him, we hear of this act of brutality towards his brother, against whom no one but he has any grudge. Do not you think there is something strange in this?"

"Yes; certainly there may be something in it," said the colonel. "I must look it up at once."

He arose, called his servant, and presently rode off at a sharp trot towards the town.

And for several days he continued to go there, to hear if the investigation had produced any result. On the fourth day he came home towards evening, and sent word to Mrs. Ritter, who was seated by Pussy's bed, that he had something important to tell her. It was that the police had been seeking for Jorg, and had found him without much delay; for he had not taken precautions to conceal himself, being sure that no one had seen him on the evening when he visited his native village. He had, therefore, merely gone to the city, and was spending his time in the taverns. When they took him into custody, and accused him, he denied every thing; but when he heard that Colonel Ritter had accusations to make against him, he was intimidated, thinking that the colonel must have seen him, or he would never have suspected him, as he had just returned from the Neapolitan army service. It never occurred to him that one single word that he had thrown to a little child had betrayed him.

When he heard the truth, he began to swear terribly, and declared he had always known that those aristocrats would bring him into trouble. On further examination, he said he had gone to his brother's house with the intention of asking him for a loan of money; but when he looked through the brilliantly lighted window and saw the big pile of money lying on the table, it occurred to him that he would strike Andrew down and rob him. He had not meant to kill him,--only render him insensible. Nearly all the money was found at his lodgings, and taken. Jorg was lodged in the prison.

When these facts were made known in the village, everybody was very much interested and excited, for nothing of the kind had happened before in that small place. In the school, particularly, every thing was topsy-turvy, for the children were as much excited as their elders. Otto scarcely stopped to take breath all day long, for he ran from one place to another, hoping to hear the latest news at each. He came to the house, on the third evening, in such a state, that his mother told him that he must sit perfectly quiet and silent for a little while before he communicated the piece of news with which he was bursting.

At last he was calm enough to tell them that they wanted to set Joggi free, for he had been shut up all this time; but the poor fellow was so convinced that they only wanted to take him out to cut off his head, that he fought against being removed with all his might. So they decided to take him out by force, and two men dragged him into the open air. He fought and screamed so violently, that a crowd soon assembled; and the poor, foolish fellow, becoming more and more alarmed, had darted away like an arrow to the nearest barn, where he took refuge from his imaginary danger in a stall, cowering down in a heap in one corner, and would not let anybody approach him. His countenance showed his terrible fear. He had been there all day and night; and now the peasant to whom the barn belonged said if he did not move soon, he would use the pitchfork to him.

"It is a sad, sad story, my children," said their mother, when Otto had finished. "Poor Joggi! how terribly he must suffer from his fear, that nobody can relieve him of, because he cannot understand what is said; and yet he is perfectly innocent of any evil deed or wish. Oh, if you had only told me what had happened that evening on the coast! Your keeping that a secret has had very, very sad consequences. Cannot we do something to comfort and reassure him again?"

Pussy was almost crying. "I will give him my red candy cock," she said, tearfully.

Otto was much disturbed, but he said, scornfully,--

"Yes; a nice present for a grown up man,--a sugar cock! You had better keep it for yourself."

After a moment he asked his mother, however, to allow Pussy to carry some food to Joggi in the barn: he had not eaten any thing for nearly two days.

His mother was more than willing, and had a basket filled at once with bread and sausage and cheese for the children, and sent them off without delay. Poor Joggi! there he was cowering in the stall, white as a sheet, and dared not stir. The children gradually drew near, and presently Otto held out his basket and showed the food, hoping to tempt Joggi.

"Come out, Joggi. See, all this is for you to eat."

There was no sign of movement.

"Do come out, or the peasant will stick his pitchfork into you."

The poor fellow gave a piteous moan, but still did not stir.

Now Pussy went quite close to him, put her mouth to his ear, and said, gently, "Do not be frightened, Joggi; they won't cut off your head. My papa will help you, and will not let anybody harm you. And see, Joggi; here is a candy cock, all red. Santa Claus sent you this on the Christmas-tree." And the little girl took the cock very carefully from her pocket, and held it out to Joggi.

This little gift had a wonderful effect. Joggi looked at his friend without fear, then at the candy cock, and presently began to laugh. It was many days since he had laughed. He rose slowly from his corner, and followed Otto out of the barn behind Pussy. When they got well out of the yard, Otto said,--

"You can take this basket, Joggi; we are going up there to our house. Your way is down yonder."

But Joggi shook his head, and followed close to Pussy's heels. They all went up the hill. Their mother watched the little procession coming, and her heart began to feel lighter; and she also noticed how the poor, foolish Joggi held his sugar cock in his hand, and laughed at it with childish satisfaction.

They all three entered the house and went into the sitting-room, where Pussy fetched a chair, and, taking the basket in her hand, beckoned Joggi to come to her; and when he was seated at the table, she spread out the bread and cheese and sausage before him, saying, very gently, "Now do eat,--eat up every bit, Joggi, and be happy again."

The poor fellow obeyed, and left no crumbs. He never relinquished his hold of the red cock, however. He held it in his left hand, and nodded and smiled at it from time to time. For bread and cheese and sausage he had often received, but a red candy cock never before.

At last he went down the hill to his cottage. With very happy looks Mrs. Ritter and Otto and Pussy followed his retreating form, and noticed that he changed the red cock from one hand to another, and had evidently forgotten his fears. Mrs. Ritter had not visited Andrew during three days. There was so much going on all the time, that she had not perceived how the time passed; and then she no longer felt the least anxiety about him. He was well cared for,--of that she was certain,--and was on the best road towards health and strength.

As soon as Colonel Ritter could go, he took the news of the arrest and imprisonment of Andrew's brother to the good carpenter, who listened to the story quietly, and said, after a while,--

"It was his will. It would have been far better for him to have asked me for a little money. I should have given it to him, but his way was ever a blow rather than a kind word."

Mrs. Ritter went down the mountain one cold, frosty morning, and went smiling to herself all the way; for she had pleasant plans and projects in her heart. Just as she opened the door of Andrew's cottage, Wiseli came out of the sitting-room. Her eyes were swollen and red. She had been crying. She gave Mrs. Ritter her hand very shyly, and ran into the kitchen, and shut the door. Mrs. Ritter had never seen Wiseli look in this way. What could have happened? She went into the sitting-room. There sat Andrew by the window. He, too, looked as if a bad piece of news had been brought to him.

"What has happened?" asked Mrs. Ritter; and forgot to say "good-morning," in her anxiety.

"Oh, oh!" sighed Andrew. "I wish that the child had never entered my house."

"Wiseli!" exclaimed his visitor. "Is it possible that Wiseli can have displeased you in any way?"

"Not that, by any means, good lady," Andrew hastened to answer. "No; she has made my home a paradise for me, and now she is going away; and it will seem so empty and lonely without her, I cannot bear it. You never could think, Mrs. Ritter, how I love that child. I cannot bear it, if they take her away. And the cousin Gotti has sent his boy twice to say that she is wanted at his house; and, since then, Wiseli has been so quiet, and cries in secret. It breaks my heart; for I see that she does not want to go there, though she says nothing, and to-morrow is the last day. I do not exaggerate, Mrs. Ritter; but I assure you I would prefer to give all that I have earned and saved for thirty years to her cousin Gotti, than have him take the child away."

"I would not think of doing that. In your place, Andrew, I would go to work another way," said Mrs. Ritter, when Andrew had finished his excited talk.

He questioned her with his eyes in silence.

"I mean in this way. All your worldly goods you will leave to some one who is very dear to you. You will take Wiseli as your adopted child; will be a father to her; she shall henceforth live in your house as your own daughter. You would like that, Andrew, would you not?"

He had listened with all his might, and his eyes grew bigger and bigger. Presently he grasped Mrs. Ritter's hand, and pressed it almost painfully. He leaned forward.

"Can that be done? Can I obtain the right to say that Wiseli is really my own child,--all my own, so that nobody will be able to take her from me again?"

"You can do all that, Andrew. And, once Wiseli is recognized as your child, no one will have the least right to her. You will be her father. And, to tell the truth, Andrew, I hoped that you might wish to do this; and therefore have kept my husband at home, in case you want to go into the city to take the necessary steps towards the adoption. You know you cannot walk, Andrew."

Andrew fairly lost his head over all this. He ran this way and that, looking for his Sunday coat; and kept asking all the time,

"Can it be true? Is it possible? To-day, did you say? May I go to-day?"

"At once," she said; and gave her hand to Andrew as she left him, to tell the colonel that all was ready for the visit to the town. "It will be better not to tell Wiseli until the evening, when every thing is settled, and you are quietly together here," she said, as she stepped out of the door. "Do not you agree with me?"

"Yes, certainly," was the answer. "I could not tell her now."

While Andrew was waiting until Colonel Ritter came for him to drive to the town, he sat trembling in every limb, and thought he could scarcely stand up, he was so happy and so excited. In about half an hour Wiseli saw, to her great surprise, the colonel's wagon drive up, stop at Andrew's door, the servant get down, come to the steps, take Andrew under the arm, and help him to get into the carriage. The child looked at it, as it passed away from the house down the road, and could not understand it at all; for the carpenter had not said any thing to her,--not even that he was going to drive. He had remained seated where he was, after Mrs. Ritter's departure, until the colonel's servant came for him; and the child had kept herself hidden all the time.

After his departure, she went into the sitting-room, and looked out of the window where Andrew always sat, and kept saying to herself, "To-day is the last day. To-morrow I must go to cousin Gotti."

Towards noon the child went into the kitchen, put every thing in order, and arranged Andrew's dinner; but he did not come, and she did not like to remove the things until he did. So she went back into the sitting-room; but the sad thought of the coming separation made her almost ill, and she said to herself, over and over, "To-morrow I must go to cousin Gotti;" and did not see, in her sadness, that the sunset was very beautiful, and betokened a still more beautiful morrow.

The child sprang to her feet when presently she heard the door opened. Andrew the carpenter stood before her with happy eyes, and with a look that Wiseli had never seen on his face. He sunk into a chair. He was overcome, but not with fatigue. At last he cried out, in a triumphant tone,--

"It is true, Wiseli! It is all really true! All the gentlemen said 'Yes,'--every one. You belong to me. I am your father. Call me 'father,' Wiseli."

Wiseli became white as a sheet. She stood staring at Andrew, but did not speak nor move.

"Oh! of course, of course," said the carpenter. "You can't understand me, I tell you all so confusedly. Now I will begin at the beginning. I have just written in the record book in the town, and you are my child now, and I am your father; and you will always stay here with me, and not go back to your cousin Gotti again. This is your home,--here with me."

Wiseli understood now. She sprang into Andrew's arms, clung round his neck, and cried, "Father, father!" They neither could speak a word after this for a long time,--too many things were crowding upon them. After a little, Wiseli felt a sudden light that seemed to break in upon her thoughts; and she exclaimed, looking up at Andrew,--

"O father! I know how it has all happened, and who has helped us."

"Who may it be, Wiseli?" asked Andrew.

"My mother."

"Your mother, child,--who do you mean? Your mother?"

And Wiseli related her dream about the beautiful garden with the red carnations, and a rose-bush on the other side, where the sun shone; and told him how her mother had taken her by the hand and showed her the garden, and said that her way led through that. And Wiseli was sure that her mother had not ceased to pray God to let her child's way be through that garden,--which was Andrew's garden, and the happiest place in the world for Wiseli.

"Do not you believe it too, father, now that you know that in my dream my mother showed me my road to your garden?"

Andrew could not answer. Big tears rolled down his face, but he smiled all the time that he wept. When, at last, he opened his mouth to speak, there came such a terrible knocking at the door, that nothing else could be heard. Open flew the door, and Otto was in the middle of the room with one leap; then he jumped over a chair, and shouted, "Hurrah! we have won, and Wiseli is delivered." Pussy came in behind him, ran at once to her friend, and said, pointing towards the door,--

"Now, Andrew, you will see what is coming for you, to celebrate your recovery."

Scarcely had she spoken, than the baker's boy came struggling through the doorway with a big tray upon his head that could scarcely come through. A good push from behind, however, helped him along, and he put the tray down on the table. Otto and Pussy had ordered the biggest cake, to be made at the baker's, that was ever known; and as it would not have been very large if it were round, they ordered it square, and it quite filled the oven when it was baked. Old Trine stood behind the baker's boy, and her big basket was at her feet. She had brought, among other delicacies, a bottle of good wine; for Mrs. Ritter declared that Andrew had, in all probability, not eaten a morsel since breakfast, and Wiseli was probably fasting also; and the child remembered the fact, now that she saw the feast that Trine spread upon the table. They all took their places, and a merry company they were. To be sure, the grand cake had to be cut in halves, and part put away, for otherwise there was not room on the table for the rest of the supper; but after that they were all more merry than ever feasters were before.

But the time went by, and Trine stood there waiting to take the children home,--it was late. Andrew said, at leave-taking,--

"To-day you have prepared a feast for me, and I thank you with all my heart; but I invite you to come here again on Sunday, and I will give you a feast,--the feast to celebrate my daughter's adoption."

And so they parted, all rejoicing over the fact of Wiseli being so happily at home with Andrew, and the children promising to come to the Sunday celebration. At the door Wiseli gave Otto her hand again, and said, "I thank you a thousand times for all your kindness to me, Otto. Cheppi never was so rude to me again after you frightened him that day. He was afraid to throw things at me. I owe it to your kindness."

"And I owe you something, Wiseli," replied Otto. "I have never had to sweep out the schoolhouse since the time you know of."

"And I thank you, too, Wiseli," said Pussy; for she would not be behind the others in her thanks.

Now every thing was quiet in the little room, and the moonlight streamed in through the window where Andrew took his seat, while Wiseli put all the supper dishes away, and made every thing neat again; then she came to him, and stood before him with folded hands.

"Father," she said, "let me say my mother's hymn aloud to you. I have always said it softly to myself; but I shall never forget it now, I am sure."

Andrew was glad to listen; and the child, raising her eyes to the stars, said, with the very deepest feeling thrilling through her heart,--

"To God you must confide   Your sorrow and your pain; He will true care provide,   And show you heaven again.

"For clouds and air and wind He points the path and way; Your   road   He'll also find,   Nor let your footsteps stray."

From this day forward the happiest cottage in the whole village was that of Andrew the carpenter, with its sunny garden. Wherever Wiseli showed herself, she received the very kindest notice from all the neighbors, much to the child's surprise. Formerly no one had noticed her particularly, but now even her cousin Gotti and his wife never passed the cottage without coming in to take her by the hand, and invite her to visit them.

This gave the child keen satisfaction, for she had always feared secretly her cousin's feelings about her adoption; so this kindness on his part freed her from all anxiety, and she could go her way peacefully. But these thoughts often rose within her, and she repeated to herself,--

"Otto and his family have always shown me kindness when I was alone in the wide world and friendless: these others are only kind to me since I am happy and have a father. I know well enough who are really my friends."

THE END.

The Codes Of Hammurabi And Moses
W. W. Davies

QTY

The discovery of the Hammurabi Code is one of the greatest achievements of archaeology, and is of paramount interest, not only to the student of the Bible, but also to all those interested in ancient history...

Religion   ISBN: *1-59462-338-4*   Pages:132

MSRP $12.95

The Theory of Moral Sentiments
Adam Smith

QTY

This work from 1749. contains original theories of conscience amd moral judgment and it is the foundation for systemof morals.

Philosophy   ISBN: *1-59462-777-0*   Pages:536

MSRP $19.95

Jessica's First Prayer
Hesba Stretton

QTY

In a screened and secluded corner of one of the many railway-bridges which span the streets of London there could be seen a few years ago, from five o'clock every morning until half past eight, a tidily set-out coffee-stall, consisting of a trestle and board, upon which stood two large tin cans, with a small fire of charcoal burning under each so as to keep the coffee boiling during the early hours of the morning when the work-people were thronging into the city on their way to their daily toil...

Childrens   ISBN: *1-59462-373-2*

Pages:84

MSRP $9.95

My Life and Work
Henry Ford

QTY

Henry Ford revolutionized the world with his implementation of mass production for the Model T automobile. Gain valuable business insight into his life and work with his own auto-biography... "We have only started on our development of our country we have not as yet, with all our talk of wonderful progress, done more than scratch the surface. The progress has been wonderful enough but..."

Biographies/   ISBN: *1-59462-198-5*

Pages:300

MSRP $21.95

The Art of Cross-Examination
Francis Wellman

QTY

I presume it is the experience of every author, after his first book is published upon an important subject, to be almost overwhelmed with a wealth of ideas and illustrations which could readily have been included in his book, and which to his own mind, at least, seem to make a second edition inevitable. Such certainly was the case with me; and when the first edition had reached its sixth impression in five months, I rejoiced to learn that it seemed to my publishers that the book had met with a sufficiently favorable reception to justify a second and considerably enlarged edition. ..

Pages:412

Reference ISBN: *1-59462-647-2*   *MSRP $19.95*

On the Duty of Civil Disobedience
Henry David Thoreau

QTY

Thoreau wrote his famous essay, On the Duty of Civil Disobedience, as a protest against an unjust but popular war and the immoral but popular institution of slave-owning. He did more than write—he declined to pay his taxes, and was hauled off to gaol in consequence. Who can say how much this refusal of his hastened the end of the war and of slavery?

Law   ISBN: *1-59462-747-9*   **Pages:48**

MSRP $7.45

Dream Psychology Psychoanalysis for Beginners
Sigmund Freud

QTY

Sigmund Freud, born Sigismund Schlomo Freud (May 6, 1856 - September 23, 1939), was a Jewish-Austrian neurologist and psychiatrist who co-founded the psychoanalytic school of psychology. Freud is best known for his theories of the unconscious mind, especially involving the mechanism of repression; his redefinition of sexual desire as mobile and directed towards a wide variety of objects; and his therapeutic techniques, especially his understanding of transference in the therapeutic relationship and the presumed value of dreams as sources of insight into unconscious desires.

Pages:196

Psychology   ISBN: *1-59462-905-6*   *MSRP $15.45*

The Miracle of Right Thought
Orison Swett Marden

QTY

Believe with all of your heart that you will do what you were made to do. When the mind has once formed the habit of holding cheerful, happy, prosperous pictures, it will not be easy to form the opposite habit. It does not matter how improbable or how far away this realization may see, or how dark the prospects may be, if we visualize them as best we can, as vividly as possible, hold tenaciously to them and vigorously struggle to attain them, they will gradually become actualized, realized in the life. But a desire, a longing without endeavor, a yearning abandoned or held indifferently will vanish without realization.

Pages:360

Self Help   ISBN: *1-59462-644-8*   *MSRP $25.45*

QTY

☐ **The Rosicrucian Cosmo-Conception Mystic Christianity** *by Max Heindel*   ISBN: *1-59462-188-8*   **$38.95**
The Rosicrucian Cosmo-conception is not dogmatic, neither does it appeal to any other authority than the reason of the student. It is: not controversial, but is: sent forth in the, hope that it may help to clear...   New Age/Religion Pages 646

☐ **Abandonment To Divine Providence** *by Jean-Pierre de Caussade*   ISBN: *1-59462-228-0*   **$25.95**
"The Rev. Jean Pierre de Caussade was one of the most remarkable spiritual writers of the Society of Jesus in France in the 18th Century. His death took place at Toulouse in 1751. His works have gone through many editions and have been republished...   Inspirational/Religion Pages 400

☐ **Mental Chemistry** *by Charles Haanel*   ISBN: *1-59462-192-6*   **$23.95**
Mental Chemistry allows the change of material conditions by combining and appropriately utilizing the power of the mind. Much like applied chemistry creates something new and unique out of careful combinations of chemicals the mastery of mental chemistry...   New Age Pages 354

☐ **The Letters of Robert Browning and Elizabeth Barret Barrett 1845-1846 vol II**   ISBN: *1-59462-193-4*   **$35.95**
by Robert Browning and Elizabeth Barrett   Biographies Pages 596

☐ **Gleanings In Genesis (volume I)** *by Arthur W. Pink*   ISBN: *1-59462-130-6*   **$27.45**
Appropriately has Genesis been termed "the seed plot of the Bible" for in it we have, in germ form, almost all of the great doctrines which are afterwards fully developed in the books of Scripture which follow...   Religion/Inspirational Pages 420

☐ **The Master Key** *by L. W. de Laurence*   ISBN: *1-59462-001-6*   **$30.95**
In no branch of human knowledge has there been a more lively increase of the spirit of research during the past few years than in the study of Psychology, Concentration and Mental Discipline. The requests for authentic lessons in Thought Control, Mental Discipline and...   New Age/Business Pages 422

☐ **The Lesser Key Of Solomon Goetia** *by L. W. de Laurence*   ISBN: *1-59462-092-X*   **$9.95**
This translation of the first book of the "Lernegton" which is now for the first time made accessible to students of Talismanic Magic was done, after careful collation and edition, from numerous Ancient Manuscripts in Hebrew, Latin, and French...   New Age/Occult Pages 92

☐ **Rubaiyat Of Omar Khayyam** *by Edward Fitzgerald*   ISBN:*1-59462-332-5*   **$13.95**
Edward Fitzgerald, whom the world has already learned, in spite of his own efforts to remain within the shadow of anonymity, to look upon as one of the rarest poets of the century, was born at Bredfield, in Suffolk, on the 31st of March, 1809. He was the third son of John Purcell...   Music Pages 172

☐ **Ancient Law** *by Henry Maine*   ISBN: *1-59462-128-4*   **$29.95**
The chief object of the following pages is to indicate some of the earliest ideas of mankind, as they are reflected in Ancient Law, and to point out the relation of those ideas to modern thought.   Religion/History Pages 452

☐ **Far-Away Stories** *by William J. Locke*   ISBN: *1-59462-129-2*   **$19.45**
"Good wine needs no bush, but a collection of mixed vintages does. And this book is just such a collection. Some of the stories I do not want to remain buried for ever in the museum files of dead magazine-numbers an author's not unpardonable vanity..."   Fiction Pages 272

☐ **Life of David Crockett** *by David Crockett*   ISBN: *1-59462-250-7*   **$27.45**
"Colonel David Crockett was one of the most remarkable men of the times in which he lived. Born in humble life, but gifted with a strong will, an indomitable courage, and unremitting perseverance...   Biographies/New Age Pages 424

☐ **Lip-Reading** *by Edward Nitchie*   ISBN: *1-59462-206-X*   **$25.95**
Edward B. Nitchie, founder of the New York School for the Hard of Hearing, now the Nitchie School of Lip-Reading, Inc, wrote "LIP-READING Principles and Practice". The development and perfecting of this meritorious work on lip-reading was an undertaking...   How-to Pages 400

☐ **A Handbook of Suggestive Therapeutics, Applied Hypnotism, Psychic Science**   ISBN: *1-59462-214-0*   **$24.95**
by Henry Munro   Health/New Age/Health/Self-help Pages 376

☐ **A Doll's House: and Two Other Plays** *by Henrik Ibsen*   ISBN: *1-59462-112-8*   **$19.95**
Henrik Ibsen created this classic when in revolutionary 1848 Rome. Introducing some striking concepts in playwriting for the realist genre, this play has been studied the world over.   Fiction/Classics/Plays 308

☐ **The Light of Asia** *by sir Edwin Arnold*   ISBN: *1-59462-204-3*   **$13.95**
In this poetic masterpiece, Edwin Arnold describes the life and teachings of Buddha. The man who was to become known as Buddha to the world was born as Prince Gautama of India but he rejected the worldly riches and abandoned the reigns of power when...   Religion/History/Biographies Pages 170

☐ **The Complete Works of Guy de Maupassant** *by Guy de Maupassant*   ISBN: *1-59462-157-8*   **$16.95**
"For days and days, nights and nights, I had dreamed of that first kiss which was to consecrate our engagement, and I knew not on what spot I should put my lips..."   Fiction/Classics Pages 240

☐ **The Art of Cross-Examination** *by Francis L. Wellman*   ISBN: *1-59462-309-0*   **$26.95**
Written by a renowned trial lawyer, Wellman imparts his experience and uses case studies to explain how to use psychology to extract desired information through questioning.   How-to/Science/Reference Pages 408

☐ **Answered or Unanswered?** *by Louisa Vaughan*   ISBN: *1-59462-248-5*   **$10.95**
Miracles of Faith in China   Religion Pages 112

☐ **The Edinburgh Lectures on Mental Science (1909)** *by Thomas*   ISBN: *1-59462-008-3*   **$11.95**
This book contains the substance of a course of lectures recently given by the writer in the Queen Street Hall, Edinburgh. Its purpose is to indicate the Natural Principles governing the relation between Mental Action and Material Conditions...   New Age/Psychology Pages 148

☐ **Ayesha** *by H. Rider Haggard*   ISBN: *1-59462-301-5*   **$24.95**
Verily and indeed it is the unexpected that happens! Probably if there was one person upon the earth from whom the Editor of this, and of a certain previous history, did not expect to hear again...   Classics Pages 380

☐ **Ayala's Angel** *by Anthony Trollope*   ISBN: *1-59462-352-X*   **$29.95**
The two girls were both pretty, but Lucy who was twenty-one who supposed to be simple and comparatively unattractive, whereas Ayala was credited, as her Bombwhat romantic name might show, with poetic charm and a taste for romance. Ayala when her father died was nineteen...   Fiction Pages 484

☐ **The American Commonwealth** *by James Bryce*   ISBN: *1-59462-286-8*   **$34.45**
An interpretation of American democratic political theory. It examines political mechanics and society from the perspective of Scotsman James Bryce   Politics Pages 572

☐ **Stories of the Pilgrims** *by Margaret P. Pumphrey*   ISBN: *1-59462-116-0*   **$17.95**
This book explores pilgrims religious oppression in England as well as their escape to Holland and eventual crossing to America on the Mayflower, and their early days in New England...   History Pages 268

QTY

The Fasting Cure by *Sinclair Upton*   ISBN: *1-59462-222-1*   **$13.95**
In the Cosmopolitan Magazine for May, 1910, and in the Contemporary Review (London) for April, 1910, I published an article dealing with my experiences in fasting. I have written a great many magazine articles, but never one which attracted so much attention... New Age/Self Help/Health Pages 164

Hebrew Astrology by *Sepharial*   ISBN: *1-59462-308-2*   **$13.45**
In these days of advanced thinking it is a matter of common observation that we have left many of the old landmarks behind and that we are now pressing forward to greater heights and to a wider horizon than that which represented the mind-content of our progenitors... Astrology Pages 144

Thought Vibration or The Law of Attraction in the Thought World   ISBN: *1-59462-127-6*   **$12.95**
by *William Walker Atkinson*   Psychology/Religion Pages 144

Optimism by *Helen Keller*   ISBN: *1-59462-108-X*   **$15.95**
Helen Keller was blind, deaf, and mute since 19 months old, yet famously learned how to overcome these handicaps, communicate with the world, and spread her lectures promoting optimism. An inspiring read for everyone... Biographies/Inspirational Pages 84

Sara Crewe by *Frances Burnett*   ISBN: *1-59462-360-0*   **$9.45**
In the first place, Miss Minchin lived in London. Her home was a large, dull, tall one, in a large, dull square, where all the houses were alike, and all the sparrows were alike, and where all the door-knockers made the same heavy sound... Childrens/Classic Pages 88

The Autobiography of Benjamin Franklin by *Benjamin Franklin*   ISBN: *1-59462-135-7*   **$24.95**
The Autobiography of Benjamin Franklin has probably been more extensively read than any other American historical work, and no other book of its kind has had such ups and downs of fortune. Franklin lived for many years in England, where he was agent... Biographies/History Pages 332

Name	
Email	
Telephone	
Address	
City, State ZIP	

☐ Credit Card   ☐ Check / Money Order

Credit Card Number	
Expiration Date	
Signature	

Please Mail to: Book Jungle
                  PO Box 2226
                  Champaign, IL 61825
or Fax to: 630-214-0564

ORDERING INFORMATION

web: *www.bookjungle.com*
email: *sales@bookjungle.com*
fax: *630-214-0564*
mail: *Book Jungle PO Box 2226 Champaign, IL 61825*
or PayPal *to sales@bookjungle.com*

Please contact us for bulk discounts

DIRECT-ORDER TERMS

20% Discount if You Order Two or More Books
Free Domestic Shipping!
Accepted: Master Card, Visa,
Discover, American Express

www.ingramcontent.com/pod-product-compliance
Lightning Source LLC
Chambersburg PA
CBHW080909020726
47502CB00008B/2405